P9-DIZ-506

"You're not helping me feel any less trapped than I already do, Aaron."

Again, he shrugged. Again, Rosa took a step forward.

"And you're not as unaffected by all this as you're pretending."

"What are you doing?" he asked, clasping her wrist just before her hand reached his face. Somehow she'd closed the distance between them as she'd said her last words without him noticing.

"I'm trying to show you that you're not as aloof as you believe," she said, and dropped her hand with a triumphant smile. "I told you."

He didn't reply. He couldn't do so without telling her that she was right, and unaffected was the *last* thing he felt. But he showed her. Slid an arm around her waist and hauled her against him.

"Maybe you're right," he said, his voice slightly breathless. "Maybe I was thinking about the first time we kissed." He dipped his head lower. "You remember."

It wasn't a question. And the way her breath quickened—the way her hand shook as she wiped the rain from her brow—confirmed it to him.

WITHDRAWN

Dear Reader,

In my 2017 release, *A Marriage Worth Saving*, I wrote my first second-chance romance. I enjoyed it so much that I revisited that theme for *Surprise Baby, Second Chance*. Rosa and Aaron's bond was created during a difficult time in their lives, but their love helped them through it. Now, faced with new challenges, they must allow their love to help them through once again...

Rosa and Aaron are characters I hope you can relate to. I wrote them that way because I want you, my readers, to know that your struggles are universal. And that, like Rosa and Aaron do, you can overcome—or at least face them—too. I'm proud to be able to write about mental health in this book, and I hope that resonates with you as much as it has with me.

If you'd like to get in touch with me, you can find me on Twitter and Facebook. You can also catch up with me on my blog.

Now I'll leave you to enjoy Rosa and Aaron's story in peace. :)

Love,

Therese

Surprise Baby, Second Chance

—

Therese Beharrie

If you purchased this book without a cover you should be aware that this book is stolen property. It was reported as "unsold and destroyed" to the publisher, and neither the author nor the publisher has received any payment for this "stripped book."

ISBN-13: 978-1-335-13525-4

Surprise Baby, Second Chance

First published in Great Britain in 2019

Copyright © 2019 by Therese Beharrie

All rights reserved including the right of reproduction in whole or in part in any form. This edition is published by arrangement with Harlequin Books S.A.

This is a work of fiction. Names, characters, places, locations and incidents are purely fictional and bear no relationship to any real life individuals living or dead, or to any actual places, business establishments, locations, events or incidents. Any resemblance is entirely coincidental.

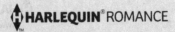

HARLEQUIN® ROMANCE

If you purchased this book without a cover you should be aware that this book is stolen property. It was reported as "unsold and destroyed" to the publisher, and neither the author nor the publisher has received any payment for this "stripped book."

Recycling programs
for this product may
not exist in your area.

ISBN-13: 978-1-335-13525-4

Surprise Baby, Second Chance

First North American publication 2018

Copyright © 2018 by Therese Beharrie

All rights reserved. Except for use in any review, the reproduction or utilization of this work in whole or in part in any form by any electronic, mechanical or other means, now known or hereafter invented, including xerography, photocopying and recording, or in any information storage or retrieval system, is forbidden without the written permission of the publisher, Harlequin Enterprises Limited, 22 Adelaide St. West, 40th Floor, Toronto, Ontario M5H 4E3, Canada.

This is a work of fiction. Names, characters, places and incidents are either the product of the author's imagination or are used fictitiously, and any resemblance to actual persons, living or dead, business establishments, events or locales is entirely coincidental.

This edition published by arrangement with Harlequin Books S.A.

For questions and comments about the quality of this book, please contact us at CustomerService@Harlequin.com.

® and TM are trademarks of Harlequin Enterprises Limited or its corporate affiliates. Trademarks indicated with ® are registered in the United States Patent and Trademark Office, the Canadian Intellectual Property Office and in other countries.

Printed in U.S.A.

Being an author has always been **Therese Beharrie**'s dream. But it was only when the corporate world loomed during her final year at university that she realized how soon she wanted that dream to become a reality. So she got serious about her writing, and now writes books she wants to see in the world featuring people who look like her for a living. When she's not writing, she's spending time with her husband and dogs in Cape Town, South Africa. She admits that this is a perfect life, and is grateful for it.

Books by Therese Beharrie

Harlequin Romance

Conveniently Wed, Royally Bound

United by Their Royal Baby
Falling for His Convenient Queen

The Tycoon's Reluctant Cinderella
A Marriage Worth Saving
The Millionaire's Redemption
Tempted by the Billionaire Next Door

Visit the Author Profile page at Harlequin.com.

Grant.
Thank you for keeping me steady through my
anxieties.

My ROSA Typewriter Club.
I'm so lucky to have found you both. Thank you
for believing in me. Always remember how much I
believe in you.

And Megan.
Thank you for your patience with me. You've taught
me so much. I can't wait for the rest of our books
together—sorry, I couldn't resist!

Praise for
Therese Beharrie

"I really enjoyed this book. It had a gutsy,
sympathetic heroine, a moody hero, and the South
African setting was vividly drawn. A great debut
novel. I'll definitely be reading this author again."

—*Goodreads* on *The Tycoon's Reluctant Cinderella*

CHAPTER ONE

ROSA SPENCER HAD two options.

One: she could get back into the taxi that had brought her to the house she was currently standing in front of.

Two: she could walk into that house and face the man she'd left four months ago without any explanation.

Her husband.

When the purr of the car grew distant behind her she took a deep breath. Her chance of escape now gone, she straightened her shoulders and walked down the pathway that led to the front door of the Spencers' holiday home.

It could have been worse, she considered. She could have bumped into Aaron somewhere in Cape Town, where she'd been staying since she'd left him. And since they'd lived together over a thousand kilometres away in Johannesburg, Rosa would have been unprepared to see him.

Since she worked from home most days, she would have probably been wearing the not-quite-pyjamas-but-might-as-well-be outfit she usually wore when she ventured out of the house during the week. Her hair would have been a mess, curls sp ralling everywhere—or piled on top of her head—and her face would have been clear of make-up.

Exposed, she thought. Vulnerable.

At least now she was prepared to see him.

Her gold dress revealed generous cleavage and cinched at her waist with a thin belt. Its skirt was long, loose, though it had a slit up to mid-thigh—stopping just before her shapewear began—to reveal a leg that was strong and toned: one of her best assets.

Her dress made her feel confident—after all, what was the point of being a designer if she couldn't make clothes that did?—as did the mass of curls around her face, and the make-up she'd had done before she'd got onto the private plane her mother-in-law had sent for her.

She hadn't seen Liana Spencer in the four months since she'd left Aaron either. And perhaps that was part of the reason Rosa had agreed to attend a birthday party that would put her face to face with the man she'd walked away from.

The other reason was because of her own mother. And the birthday parties Violet Lang would never get to celebrate.

Rosa took another breath, clinging to the confidence she'd fought for with her dress. It was a pivotal part of the armour she'd created when she'd realised she'd be seeing Aaron again.

She needed the armour to cloak the shivering in the base of her stomach. The erratic beating of her heart. The combination of the two was so familiar that she didn't think she'd ever truly lived without it. Though that hadn't stopped her from running from it all her life.

The door of the house was open when she got there and Rosa slipped inside, thinking that it would be easier than to announce her arrival by ringing the bell. There was nothing to indicate a celebration on the first floor—just the usual tasteful but obviously expensive furniture and décor—though that wasn't surprising. Liana usually went for lavish, which meant the top floor. The one where the walls were made entirely of glass.

It offered guests an exceptional view of the sea that surrounded Mariner's Island just off the coast of Cape Town. Of the waves that crashed against the rocks that were scattered at the beach just a few metres from the Spencer house. And of the small town and airport that stood only a short distance away from the house too.

Rosa held her breath as she got to the top of the stairs, and then pushed open the door before she lost her nerve.

And immediately told herself that she should have escaped when she had the chance.

There was no party on this floor. Instead, it looked like it usually did when there were no events planned. There was a living area and a bed on one side of the room—the bathroom being the only section of the floor with privacy—and a dining area and kitchen on the other side.

There was an open space between the two sides as if whoever had designed the room had decided to give the Spencers an area to be free in.

But in that open space stood her husband. *Only* her husband.

And the last thing Rosa thought of was freedom.

His back was to her, and she thought that she still had the chance to escape. He didn't know that she was there. If she left he wouldn't ever have to know. What harm would it do?

Except that when she turned back to the door it was closed. And when she looked over her shoulder to see if he'd noticed her she saw that Aaron was now facing her, an unreadable expression on his face.

'Running?'

'N-no.' *Be confident.*

His mouth lifted into a half-smile. 'No?' he asked in a faintly mocking tone.

Her face went hot. The shivering intensified. Her heart rate rocketed. But, despite that, she was able to offer him a firm, 'No'.

'Okay,' he replied in a voice that told her he didn't believe her. And why would he? Hadn't she run from him before? Without the decency to explain why? Hadn't the anxiety of that decision kept her up night after night?

Guilt shimmered through her.

She ignored it.

But ignoring it meant that her brain had to focus on something else. And—as it usually did—it chose his face.

Her eyes feasted on what her memories hadn't done justice to over the last four months. His dark hair, dark brows, the not-quite-chocolate colour of his skin. The mixture of his Indian and African heritage had created an arresting face, his features not unlike those Rosa had seen on movie stars.

But his face had more than just good looks. It spoke of the cool, calm demeanour that had always exasperated her even as it drew her in. He rarely let his emotions out of wherever he kept them, so they seldom claimed the planes of his face.

Except when he and Rosa were having a conversation about their feelings. Or when they were making love. There'd been nothing *but* emotion on his face then.

'Where is everybody?' she asked in a hoarse voice.

Aaron slid his hands into his pockets, making his biceps bulge slightly under the material of his suit jacket. Her breath taunted her as it slipped out of her lungs. As it reminded her that it wasn't only Aaron's face that she was attracted to.

It was his muscular body. It was how much taller than her he was. It was his broad shoulders, the strength of his legs, of everything in between.

He'd always been thrilled by the curves of her

body. But his hands were large enough, strong enough, that she'd always thought he wouldn't have wanted her as much if her curves hadn't been as generous.

Aaron took a step towards her.

Which was no reason for her to move back.

But she did.

'Well, if I'm right—and I probably am—everyone's here who's supposed to be.'

'I don't understand. It's just you and...' She trailed off, her heart thudding. 'Did you—did you do this?'

'Oh, no,' Aaron replied, and took another step towards her. This time she managed to keep her feet in place. 'Why would I want to see the wife who left me with no explanation?'

'Great. Then I'll go.'

She turned to the door again, ignoring her confusion. She'd figure it out when she was off the island that reminded her so much of her husband.

The island where he'd taken her months after her mother had died. Where he'd got down on one knee. Where he'd told her he couldn't imagine life without her.

Where they'd spent time after their wedding. Lounging in the sun at the beach. Lazily enjoying each other's bodies as only newlyweds could.

Where they'd taken holidays. When life had become too much for her and Aaron had surprised her with a trip away.

The island where he'd held her, comforted her, loved her on the bed that stood in the corner, its memories haunting her. Overwhelming her.

Yes, she'd figure it all out when she was away from the island. And far, *far* away from her husband.

A hand pressed against the door before she could open it. She swallowed and then turned back to face him.

Her heart sprinted now. Her body prickled. The scent of his masculine cologne filled her senses. Memories, sharp and intimate, could no longer be held back.

Again, she tried to ignore them. But it was becoming harder to do.

'Why are you stopping me from leaving?' she managed in a steady voice.

'Did you think you were just going to walk in here, see me, and then…leave?'

'I thought I was attending your mother's sixtieth birthday party.'

'Which I would have been at too.'

'And we would have seen each other there, yes. But you're the only one here. I've seen you. Now I want to leave.'

'Just like that?'

'Just like that.'

He inched closer. 'You're not the slightest bit curious about why you and I are alone here?'

'Sure I am. But I'm also pretty sure I can figure it out on my way to the airport.'

'The airport?' His lips curved into a smile. 'Honey, the airport's closed.'

'No,' she said after a beat. 'No, it can't be. I just got off a plane. Your mother said it would be waiting for me when I was done here.'

His smile faded. 'She lied. Your flight is likely to be the last one until Monday. The airport's closed this weekend.'

Panic thickened in her throat. '*All* weekend?'

'Don't sound so surprised, Rosa,' he said mildly. 'You know Mariner's Island doesn't work the way the rest of the world does.'

'Yes, but…but it was a *private* plane. Yours.'

'It still needs somewhere to take off from. To land at. And since the airport's closed we won't have that until Monday.'

She ducked under his arm, put distance between them. But it didn't make breathing any easier. 'So… what? Your mother just decided to leave her guests stranded here until Monday?'

'Not guests,' he corrected. 'Just you and me.'

'Did you know about this?'

'No.'

'Then how did you not suspect something was off when the main route off the island would only be viable again on *Monday*?'

'She told me that the party would be going on for most of the weekend.'

'And you *believed* her?'

'Yes,' he said coldly. 'It's not unusual for one of

my mother's parties to continue for an entire weekend. You know that.'

'Okay,' she said, and lifted the curls off her forehead with a shaky hand. 'Okay, fine.' Her hand dropped. 'Then I'll take a boat home.'

'It's too late to get one tonight.'

'I know,' she said through clenched teeth. 'I'll take one tomorrow morning.'

'There's a storm warning for tomorrow. Starting tonight, actually.'

She looked beyond the glass walls, saw the dark clouds rolling in. Her stomach tumbled. 'That's fine.'

'It'll be a rough storm, Rosa. It's anticipated to last until tomorrow evening at least. Do you still want to take a boat?'

'Yes.'

He laughed softly. 'You're so determined to get away from me you'll take an almost two-hour boat ride in a storm? Even though you get sick when the water is calm?'

She hesitated. 'I'll be fine.'

His half-smile mocked her. 'I'm sure you will be.'

He was right, she thought, and hated herself for admitting it. Hated him for being right.

Except that what she felt in that moment was anything *but* hate.

Confusion, yes. How had this happened? Had Liana really orchestrated this on purpose?

Guilt, of course. She'd walked away from him. From their relationship. She hadn't even said goodbye.

Anger, *absolutely*. She *hated* feeling trapped. It reminded her of her childhood. Of being caught in her mother's world.

But hate? No, she thought, her eyes settling on Aaron again. There was no hate.

'Why are you so calm?'

'I'm not,' he replied in a tone that gave no indication that he wasn't. 'But I know my mother. And I know this scheme is probably well-thought-out. Much like the first time we met. Or don't you remember?' His voice was soft, urgent. 'Have you run away from the memories too, Rosa?'

She didn't reply. There was no reply she could give. She couldn't tell him that she hadn't been running away from him, not really, but *saving* him. From the anxiety, the stress, the worry of being with someone who was terrified of losing the health of their mind, their body.

Rosa had spent her life looking after someone like that. She knew the anxiety, the stress, the worry of it. She knew the guilt when the fear became a reality.

She'd saved him, she thought again. She'd saved him from going through what she'd gone through with her mother's hypochondria. She'd saved him from having to take care of another person. From having it break him.

The moment she'd felt that lump in her breast, she'd known she couldn't put him through all of that. So she'd walked away. Had tried to move on.

But the memories wouldn't let her. No, the memories were always, *always* there.

'Great,' Rosa said loudly. 'No one's here.'

But that didn't make sense. Her mother had told her there was a Christmas ball for cancer patients that night. Had asked Rosa to be her partner at the ball.

Of course, Rosa had agreed. Her father wasn't in Cape Town, though she doubted he would have agreed to accompany her mother even if he had been. Irritation bristled over her, but she forced her attention to the matter at hand. She'd spent enough of her time being annoyed at her father.

The room was decorated as if there was supposed to be a ball. A large crystal chandelier hung in the middle of the ceiling, white draping flowing from it to different spots on the walls. It lit the space with soft light, brightened only by the small Christmas trees in each corner of the room that had been adorned with twinkling lights.

There was only one table at the end of the room, standing next to the largest Christmas tree Rosa had ever seen, with champagne, canapés and desserts spread across it.

'Am I early?' Rosa wondered out loud again.

But, like the first time, she got no response.

Throwing her hands up, she turned to try and find someone who could explain what was happening. As she took a step towards the door, it opened and her breathing did something strange when a man joined her in the room.

'Who are you?' she blurted out.

He lifted an eyebrow. 'Aaron Spencer. Who are you?'

'Rosa Lang.' She swallowed. How had the air around her suddenly become so charged? 'I'm, um, here for the Christmas ball...'

'Me too.' His eyes lazily scanned the room. 'Either we're really early or—'

'Or our mothers have decided to play a game on us,' Rosa said, his name suddenly registering with her.

He was Liana Spencer's son. Rosa had only met the woman a few times during her mother's group chemotherapy sessions but she'd been charmed. Not only by the woman's energy—which she envied greatly—but because she'd done an amazing job at keeping Rosa's mother's energy up, despite the fact that she was going through chemo too.

Liana had been vocal about wanting Rosa to meet her son, and Violet had tried to get Rosa to agree to it just as passionately. The dress Liana had sent her—along with the make-up, hair and car she'd arranged—began to make more sense. And seeing Aaron now had Rosa regretting that she'd resisted an introduction for such a long time...

'I wouldn't put it past my mother,' Aaron replied darkly. It sent a shiver down her spine. But she didn't know if that was because of what he'd said or the fact that she felt inexplicably drawn to him. Even though he didn't seem quite as enamoured.

'This does seem like an excessive prank though.'

'My mother's speciality.'

'Really?' She tilted her head and, for once, let herself lean into what she wanted to do, refusing to give the doubt that followed her around constantly any footing. 'How about we have a glass of champagne and you can tell me all about it?'

She wasn't sure how long he studied her. But when his lips curved into a smile—when his expression turned from reserved into one she couldn't describe but *felt*, deep in her stomach—she knew she would have waited an eternity for it. And thought that—just maybe—he was drawn to her too…

'I remember,' Rosa said softly. 'It was a hospital Christmas ball. Or so we thought. Our mothers told us they wanted us to go with them. That they'd meet us there because they wanted to have dinner before. But there was no hospital Christmas ball. Just a party for two that our mothers had arranged so that we could meet.'

There was a tenderness on Rosa's face that didn't fit with the woman who'd left him four months ago. An indulgence too, though he suspected that was for her mother who'd passed away a year after that incident. And for his mother, who Rosa still had a soft spot for, despite what she'd seen Liana put him through over the years.

Aaron clenched his jaw. The emotion might have been misleading but her actions hadn't been. She'd left him without a word. Without a phone call. Without a note. He'd got home from work one day to find her clothes gone. She'd taken nothing else, and he'd had to face living in the house they'd furnished together—the home they'd *built* together—alone.

'I imagine my mother wanted this to be much the same,' Aaron said curtly. 'She forces us to be alone together but, instead of starting to date this time, we work things out.'

'But it's not like before,' she denied. 'There actually was a ball then. Sure, no one else was there, but there was food and drink, and the place had been decorated for a party. This—' she gestured around them '—is so far away from that.'

'But she sent you a dress again?' He tried to keep what seeing her in that dress did to him out of his voice.

'No. I designed this one.'

'You've never made anything like this for yourself before.'

'I know. It was…a special occasion. Your mom's sixtieth birthday,' she added quickly. But it was too late. He'd already figured out that she'd made the dress because of him.

He wasn't sure if he was pleased or annoyed by the fact. He'd been trying to get her to make something for herself for years. Now, when they were…whatever they were, she'd chosen to listen to him.

Perhaps that was why she'd left. Because he'd been holding her back. He'd add it to the list of possibilities. A list that spoke loudly—accusingly—of his faults.

'I'm sure she would have if you hadn't told her you'd sort yourself out,' he said to distract himself. 'And she arranged the plane for you. And the car to get you here. She's a regular old fairy godmother,' he added dryly.

'No. No,' she said again. 'That can't be it. She wouldn't have arranged all of this just to play at being a fairy godmother.'

'She did it before. When we met.'

'That was just as much my mom as it was yours.'

'Somehow, I think my mother had more to do with it.' His shoulders tightened. 'She likes to think she doesn't live in the real world. And now, with this, she gets to play the perfect role. The good guy. The fairy godmother. To orchestrate a happy ever after.'

'For you and me?'

'Who else?' he asked sharply, hating the surprise in her voice. She winced, stepped back, brushed at her hair again. It spiralled around her face in that free and slightly wild way her curls dictated.

'You're saying your mother tricked us into being here together because she wants us to…reconcile?' He nodded. 'Why?'

'I don't know,' he said sarcastically. 'Maybe because we were happily married until I got home one day to find you'd disappeared?' She blanched. 'Or maybe I'd fooled myself into believing we were happy.'

She bit her lip, looked away. 'Did she tell you that she wanted us to have a happy ever after?'

He gritted his teeth, then forced himself to relax. Control was key. 'Not directly. But she's been urging me to contact you for the last four months.' He cocked his head. 'How did *she* contact you?'

'My…email. I've been checking my emails.'

Tension vibrated between them. As did the unspoken words.

I've been checking my emails. I just haven't replied to yours.

'I was always going to attend her birthday, Aaron,' Rosa said softly. 'You know this is about more than your mother. More than you and me.'

He did. Rosa's mother had made his mother promise to celebrate each birthday with vigour. A reminder that they'd lived. That they'd had a *life*.

That had been a deathbed promise.

It angered him even more that his mother would use her birthday as an opportunity for her scheme.

In all the years she'd manipulated situations—in all the years she'd blamed her 'zest for life' for interfering in other people's lives—she'd never done anything this...*conniving*.

And in all the years since he'd taken responsibility for Liana since he'd realised she wouldn't take responsibility herself, Aaron had never felt more betrayed.

Or perhaps the betrayal he felt about Rosa leaving was intensifying his reaction.

Whatever it was, he wouldn't allow it to control him any more. He walked to the door...and cursed when he found it locked.

CHAPTER TWO

'WHAT?' ROSA ASKED, anxiety pounding with her heart. 'What is it?'

'It's locked.'

'It's—what?' She strode past him and tried the handle of the door. It turned, but no amount of pressure made it open. 'No,' she said, shaking her head. 'This is not happening. We are *not* locked in here. There must be some mistake.'

Panic spurred her movements and she reached into the clutch she'd forgotten was in her hand. She took her phone out. 'I have signal!' she said triumphantly. 'Only a few bars, but it should work. Who should I call?'

'I suppose we could try the police.' His calm voice was a stark contrast to the atmosphere around them.

'Do you have the number?'

'No.'

She stared at him. 'How do you not have the number of the police?'

'It's on my phone. It's dead,' he said, nodding in the direction of the table where it lay.

'You didn't charge it,' she said with a sigh. It was something he did—or didn't do—regularly. Which had driven her crazy on good days. This day had been anything but good.

But if he was going to pretend to be calm—if he was going to pretend he wasn't freaking out when she knew that he was—she could too.

'Okay, so we don't have the number for the police station. I'm assuming that covers all emergency services?' He nodded. 'I guess we better hope that nothing happens during this storm,' she muttered, and scanned her contacts for the number she was looking for.

As if in response to her words, a streak of lightning whipped across the sky. It was closely followed by booms of thunder. Rosa closed her eyes and brought the phone to her ear.

'Liana, we're locked in,' Rosa said the moment she heard Liana's voice—distant, crackling—on the phone.

'Rosa?'

'Yes, it's Rosa. Aaron and I are trapped on the top floor of the house.'

'What?' Static dulled the sound of Liana's voice even more. 'Did you get to the house safely?'

'I'm fine. But we're locked in, so we can't get off the top floor.'

Liana didn't reply and Rosa looked at the phone to see if they'd been cut off, but the call was still ongoing.

'Here, let me try,' Aaron said and she handed him the phone. And bit back the response that *him* speaking to his mother couldn't magically make the connection better.

'Mom? We're locked on the top floor of the house. Hello? *Hello?*'

Rosa waited as Aaron fell silent, and then he looked at the display on the phone and sighed. 'It cut off. I don't think she got any of that.'

'We could try someone else—'

She broke off when thunder echoed again, this time followed by a vicious flash of lightning. And then everything went dark.

'Aaron?'

'Yeah, I'm here.'

Her panic ebbed somewhat with the steadiness of his voice. 'Does this mean what I think it means?'

'Yeah, the power went out.' She heard movement, and then the light of her phone shone between them. 'The generator should be kicking in soon though.'

Silence spread between them as they waited.

And relief took the place of tension when the lights flickered on again.

'I think we're going to be stuck here for a while,' Aaron said after a moment.

'We could just try calling someone again.'

'Who?'

'Look up the number for the police,' she snapped. Sucked in a breath. Told herself her confident façade was slipping. Ignored the voice in her head telling her it had slipped a long time ago.

Aaron didn't reply and tapped on the screen of the phone. Then he looked up. 'There's no signal. It must have something to do with the electricity being out.'

'That's impossible. We can't *not* have a connection.'

'It's Mariner's Island,' he said simply, as though it explained everything.

And, if she were honest with herself, it did. Mariner's Island was tiny. The locals who lived and worked there did so for the sake of tourism. And it was the perfect tourist destination. In the summer. When the demands on power and the likelihood of storms were low.

There was a reason the airport had closed over the weekend. A reason the lights had gone out. The island thrived during summer, but survived during winter.

A clap of thunder punctuated her thoughts and she turned in time to see another flash of lightning streak across the sky. She badly wanted to try the door again, but when she turned back she saw Aaron watching her. And if she tried the door again she would be proving him right. She would be proving to him that she *was* running. She would look like a fool.

She didn't want to look like a fool. A fool desperate not to be in the same room with the husband she'd left.

With the husband she still loved.

* * *

Again, Aaron found himself enthralled by the emotion on her face. She looked torn, though he didn't know between what.

It wasn't the ideal situation, them being locked in this room together. But it was what it was. And, since the storm was probably going to keep the good folk of Mariner's Island in their homes, no one would be saving them for a while.

They'd have to accept that fact and do the best that they could.

It almost seemed as if he were okay with it. As if being alone with the woman who'd left him wouldn't remind him of all the reasons he'd given himself for why she'd left.

His reluctance to be spontaneous. His caution surrounding their lives. How he always had to clean up the messes his mother created. How he did so without a word.

She hadn't seemed to mind any of it before. But then she'd left, so what did he know?

'You should turn your phone off.'

'What? Why?'

'Preserve the battery.' He took off his jacket, loosened his tie. Threw them both over the couch. 'We're not calling anyone for a while, but we'll have to do so tomorrow.'

'But what if someone tries to contact us?'

'No one is going to contact us.'

He opened the top button of his shirt, and then

narrowed his eyes when he saw two suitcases in the corner of the room. He'd known something was up when he'd got to the top floor and saw that it hadn't been set up for a party. Instead, it looked as it usually did when they visited normally.

Perhaps that had dulled his suspicions. He'd thought his mother had wanted them to share a meal, or that they'd meet there before going to the actual party.

He should have known better.

The pieces had only fallen into place when he'd seen Rosa. And he'd barely managed to see the whole picture those pieces painted when he'd been battling the emotion at seeing her again.

He walked over to the cases and laid them both on the bed. The first held men's clothing. The second, women's.

'Is that *lingerie*?'

His lips twitched. 'Yes.'

She'd come over from where she'd been standing on the opposite side of the bed and now began to throw the offending items out of the case. 'Well, at least there are some other things here too.' She paused. 'Did your mother pack this?'

He shrugged.

'The other things—' she pulled out a casual-looking dress, holding it between her index finger and thumb '—are less…seductive, I suppose. But I don't think any of them would fit me.' She frowned.

'If it was your mother, this makes no sense. She knows what size I am.'

'Maybe the selection was meant to seduce anyway.' He fought to steady his voice. 'You'd be able to wear that, but it would be tighter than what you're used to. Or more uncomfortable. So you'd—'

'Be encouraged to wear the lingerie?'

'I was going to say you'd look different.' He said the words deliberately now, determined not to show her how the conversation was messing with his head.

'There's nothing wrong with how I usually dress.'

'No,' he agreed.

'So…what? Tighter, more uncomfortable—*different*—clothing would seduce you? And then we'd reunite.' She said the last words under her breath, as though saying them to herself. 'There isn't anything I can wear here that's appropriate for this.' She gestured around them.

'I don't think my mother intended this.'

'Us being trapped?'

He nodded. 'She probably wanted us to go out and enjoy the island like we have in the past.' He let that sit for a moment. 'You're free to use whatever she's packed for me.'

'It'll probably only be jeans and shirts.'

You could wear the lingerie, if you like.

The words seared his brain. Out loud, he said, 'You're welcome to help yourself.'

He walked to the other side of the room, as though somehow the distance would keep him from remembering her in lingerie. And what had happened after he'd seen her in lingerie. It would do nothing for his need for control to remember that.

He eyed the alcohol his mother had left on the counter of the kitchen—at least she'd done *that*—and reached for the rum and soda water, adding ice from the freezer. He was sipping it when he faced her again, but her back was towards him and the memories he'd tried to suppress struggled free, even though he couldn't see her front.

But he didn't need to.

Because, from where he stood, he could see the strong curve of her shoulders, the sweeping slope of her neck. He'd only have to press a kiss there, have his tongue join, and she would moan. She'd grab his hands as his mouth did its work and pull them around her, over her breasts, encouraging him to touch them...

He gritted his teeth. Reminded himself—again—that he needed to be in control. But his reaction wasn't a surprise. His attraction to Rosa had always goaded him in this way. When he'd first seen her—her curves, the curls around her face, the golden-brown of her skin—it had kicked him in the gut.

He'd managed to ignore it for a full year, and only because both their mothers had been going through chemotherapy and acting on his attraction had seemed inappropriate. But their year of friendship hadn't been enough for him. And their chemistry had constantly reminded him of its presence.

Stalking him. Mocking him.

It was why control was so important now. He couldn't act on his attraction this time. He couldn't show Rosa how much she'd hurt him when she'd left. And how shaken he was to see her again. He'd only just begun to face the fact that the morning she'd left might have been the last time he'd ever see her…

Control meant that he had a plan. And plans were how he lived his life. How he made sure his law firm remained successful. How he tried to make sure his mother hadn't created another problem for him to fix.

He hadn't had a plan in his marriage, and he'd wondered if that had contributed to how—and why—it had ended so abruptly.

Or had his need to plan been the cause of its end?

He took a long drag from his drink and shook the feelings away. He might not know if his plans—his need for control—had contributed to Rosa leaving, but having a plan was the only way he'd survive the night.

Now he just had to come up with one.

CHAPTER THREE

'DO YOU HAVE any intention of offering me a drink?' Rosa asked when she turned back and saw Aaron sipping from a glass. It was filled with golden liquid, the kind she was pretty sure would help steady the nerves fluttering in her stomach.

'What do you want?' he asked flatly.

She almost winced. 'Whatever you're having is fine.'

He nodded and went about making her drink. She walked towards him cautiously and then busied herself with putting the bottles from the counter into the cabinet beneath. It wasn't necessary, but it was a way to keep her hands busy. Especially since something about his expression made her want to do something remarkably different with her hands.

Or was that because the clothing—the lingerie— had reminded her of all the times she'd *wanted* to seduce him? Of all the times it had worked?

Her hands shook and she waited for them to steady before she packed the last bottle away.

'You don't have to do that.'

'I know.'

But I was thinking about all the times we made love and I needed a distraction.

'Do you think your mother left something for us to eat?'

'Try the fridge.'

She did, though she wasn't hungry. Again, it was just because she wanted something to do. To distract from the ache in her body. From the ache in her heart.

She found the fridge fully stocked.

'How nice of her,' Rosa said wryly. Her patience with Liana had dropped dramatically after the seductive clothing thing. And now, finding the fridge filled with food, she couldn't deny that Liana had planned this any more.

She'd indulged Liana over the years she'd got to know the woman. Understandably, she thought, considering Liana's history with her mother. With *her*, during Violet's declining health. And...after.

But Rosa had let that influence her view of Liana's actions. Actions that Rosa had condoned by not speaking out. She wouldn't let that happen again—once they got out of their current situation.

'It's full?'

'Yeah.' The hairs on her neck stood when Aaron moved in behind her to look for himself. 'There's this dish—' she took it out, handed it to him—anything to get him away from her '—which I assume is something readymade for this evening. And the rest is ingredients to make meals. Eggs, vegetables, that sort of thing.'

'There was some meat in the freezer.'

Rosa closed the fridge. 'She's thought of everything, hasn't she?'

'She generally does,' Aaron said and handed her the drink. She braced herself for the contact, but it didn't help. A spark flared anyway. She'd never really been able to come to terms with the attraction she felt for him. That she'd felt for him since day one.

Or with your love for him, a voice whispered in her head, reminding her of why she'd had to leave—before either of those things had tempted her into staying.

Staying wouldn't have done either of them any good.

'She just doesn't think about consequences.'

'Oh, I think she knows.' She removed the foil that covered the top of the dish and found a rice and chicken meal of some kind. She took out two plates and, without asking him if he wanted any, dished portions for both of them. 'That there are consequences, I mean.'

'But she never stops to consider *what* those consequences might be.' His voice was steady, but there was frustration there. He'd never been able to hide it completely when he was talking about his mother. 'You know how many times I've had to deal with consequences that weren't favourable. Like the time she gave her car to a guy she met at a conference she attended.'

Rosa nodded. 'She thought it would be easier for

him to get to his job in the city if he had a car. And that would make sure he didn't lose his job, and that he'd be able to look after his family.'

'Instead, the man *still* lost his job because *he couldn't drive*, and he ended up selling the car, which then got him into trouble with the police because she hadn't transferred the car into his name.'

'And you had to sort it all out,' she said softly. The microwave sounded, and she handed Aaron the heated plate before putting in her own. 'I'm sorry, ba—'

She stopped herself. She'd been about to call him 'baby'. And it wouldn't have been like the 'honey' he'd called her when she'd first tried to leave. No, that had been said sardonically. This? This would have been said lovingly. Endearingly.

It was because of the routine she'd slipped into. Dishing for him, heating his food. Normal parts of what had been their life before. But that life was gone. She'd walked away from it. It didn't matter why or how—she *had*. Which meant accepting that she couldn't just *slip* back into routine.

The microwave finished heating her food and she used it as an excuse to turn her back to him. To ignore the emotion that was swirling inside her.

'You didn't change,' he said into the silence that had settled in the room. She took her plate and drink to the couch and tried to figure out how to sit down without the slit revealing her leg.

'No,' she replied after a moment, and then gave

up and lowered to the seat. She set her food on the coffee table in front of them, covered as much leg as she could and then took a long sip of the drink before she answered him. 'As I predicted, there were only a couple of shirts in there and jeans. The jeans wouldn't fit me.'

He settled at the opposite end of the couch. 'You could have worn one of the shirts.'

She lifted a brow. 'And that wouldn't have been...distracting?'

'What you're wearing now isn't?'

His eyes lowered to the leg she'd been trying to cover, and then moved up to her cleavage.

'I'll go change,' she said in a hoarse voice, setting her drink down.

'No, you don't have to.'

His gaze lifted to her face, though his expression didn't do anything to help the flush that was slowly making its way through her body.

'It's probably for the best.'

'Are you afraid I'll do something neither of us wants?'

'No.'

Because both of us would want it.

'I just think it would be better for us not to... cross any boundaries.'

'Are there boundaries?' he asked casually, though she wasn't fooled by it. She could hear the danger beneath the façade. 'I didn't realise a married couple had boundaries.'

'That's not quite what we are now, though.'

'No? Did I miss the divorce papers you sent to me while you were in Cape Town?'

Bile churned in her stomach. 'There are no divorce papers.' She frowned. 'You knew where I was?'

He nodded. 'I needed to make sure you were okay.'

She closed her eyes. 'I'm sorry. I didn't think—'

'That I'd want to know that you were alive?'

'I took my clothes. I thought—' She broke off as shame filled her. 'I should have let you know.'

A chill swept over her as she took in his blank expression. 'You said we aren't *quite* married, but you haven't asked for a divorce.' He stopped, though she clearly heard the *yet* he hadn't said. 'Which is it, Rosa?'

And, though his expression was still clear of emotion, the danger in his voice was coming out in full now. She swallowed and reached for her drink again.

'I don't want to get into this,' she said after she'd taken another healthy sip. She'd need a refill soon if she went on like this.

'You can't get out of it. We're stuck here.'

'I know.' Couldn't forget it if she tried. 'I also know that if we start talking about this stuff, being trapped here is going to be a lot harder than it needs to be.'

'Stuff,' he repeated softly. Her eyes met his and

she saw the anger there. 'Is that what you call leaving me after five years of being together? After three years of marriage?'

'I call it life,' she replied sharply. 'Life happened, and I had to go.' She stood. 'There's no point in rehashing it now.'

He stood with her, and the body she'd always loved cast a shadow over her. 'Where are you going to go, Rosa?' he asked. 'There's nowhere to run. This room is open-plan. The only other room is the bathroom, and even then you wouldn't be able to stay there for ever.'

She took a step back. Lowered to the couch slowly. 'You're taking too much joy from this.'

'This isn't joy.' He sat back down, though his body didn't relax. She nearly rolled her eyes. What did he think he was going to have to do? Tackle her if she tried to get past him?

'What would you call it then?'

'Satisfaction. Karma.'

'Karma?' she said with a bark of laughter. 'I didn't realise you believed in karma.'

'I didn't. Until today. Now. When it's become clear how much you want to run from this—from me—and can't.'

Now she did roll her eyes. 'And what are *you* paying for? What did *you* do that was so bad that you deserve to be locked in a room with the wife who left you?'

His features tightened. 'Maybe I don't believe in karma then.'

'Sounds like you're taking the easy way out.'

'Or like I'm doing whatever the hell suits me.' His voice was hard, and surprise pressed her to ask what she'd said that had upset him.

But she didn't. She didn't deserve to know.

'Doing whatever the hell suits you *does* sound like you're enjoying this.'

'Maybe I am. Hard to tell since I've forced myself not to feel anything since you left.'

And there it was. The honesty, the vulnerability that had always seeped past the coolness he showed the world. The emotion that showed her how deeply he cared, even when he pretended he didn't.

It had always managed to penetrate whatever wall she'd put up with him. Or whatever wall he'd put up to make her believe he didn't feel. But he did. Which made her actions so much worse.

She'd done many stupid things in her life. Most of them because she'd wanted to find out who she was after giving so much of herself to her mother.

Like dropping out of college because she didn't think they were teaching her what she needed to know about design.

Like moving out when she was tired of being responsible for her mother's mental health.

Like ignoring her mother's phone calls for almost two months after she moved out, because she thought Violet was trying to manipulate her into coming back home. When really her mother had been calling to tell her about her cancer.

She hadn't thought anything about her relationship with Aaron had been stupid. At least she hadn't until she'd found the lump. Until it had reminded her of how stupid she'd been by choosing not to be tested for breast cancer when her mother's doctors had advised it.

And suddenly all the uncertainty she'd battled with in the past about her decisions had returned. Maybe they'd never really gone away. And the disaster scenario of what that lump could mean had echoed her mother's own anxieties so closely that it had reminded Rosa that she was her mother's child.

It would have been selfish of her to stay. To put Aaron through what she'd gone through with her mother. To put him through anything that would cause him to suffer as he had when his mother had been ill.

'Maybe that's for the best,' she told him, kicking off her shoes. 'If we don't feel anything, we don't get hurt. And since we're already in this situation—' she waved between them '—committing ourselves to not getting hurt doesn't sound so bad, does it?'

He stared at her. 'Are you...are you serious?'

'Yes,' she said, and lifted the plate she'd set on the table, resting it on her lap as she leaned back into the couch. 'Doesn't it sound appealing to you? Us not hurting each other?'

'Is that why you left? Because I hurt you?'

She toyed with the food on her plate. 'No,' she said, lifting her gaze to his. 'You didn't hurt me.'

'Then why did you leave?'

'Because I would be hurting you by staying.'

'Why?' But she shook her head. 'Rosa, you can't just tell me something like that and not give me *anything* else.' Still, she didn't answer him. He clenched his jaw. 'You don't think you're hurting me now? With *this*?'

'I know I am.'

'And that doesn't mean anything to you?'

'It…can't.'

He wanted to shout. To demand answers from her. But that would only keep her from talking to him.

And he needed her to talk to him. He needed to know why she was saying things his wife never would have said. The Rosa he'd married would never have given up on anything. She would never have settled for backing away from the possibility of pain when there was a possibility for joy.

Or perhaps this was karma, like he'd said. Maybe this was *his* karma. For not acting with reason when it came to Rosa. She'd only been twenty-three when they'd married. He'd been twenty-six. Older. Wiser.

At least old enough to know that she might not

have been ready to marry him. She'd still been grieving for her mother when he'd proposed. Her decision might not have been entirely thought through.

But as he thought back to the moment he'd proposed he couldn't remember any hesitation from Rosa…

He wanted everything to be perfect. Simple but perfect. That was his plan. And, since only he and Rosa were on the beach in front of the house on Mariner's Island, there'd be no one but himself to blame if everything didn't go perfectly.

He took a deep breath and Rosa looked up at him. 'Are you okay?'

'Yeah.'

'You're sure?' Her brow furrowed. 'Because you've been quiet since we got here. I mean, quieter than usual.'

She gave him a small smile and his heart tumbled. Even her smile could make his heart trip over itself. No wonder he was proposing to her when he'd never thought he'd get married.

'I'm thinking.'

'About?'

'This. Us.'

'Really?' She pressed in closer at his side when the wind nipped at their skin. It was cooler than he would have liked, but he supposed that was what he got by wanting to propose just as the sun was going down on an autumn day. 'And what have you come up with?'

'You're amazing.'

His feet stopped, though they weren't close to the place where he'd planned on proposing. This was good enough. Waves were crashing at their feet. Sand around them. The sun shining over them as though it approved of his actions.

Besides, none of that mattered anyway. Not any more. All that mattered was her. And that he couldn't imagine another moment going by without knowing that she'd one day be his wife.

'Well, yeah,' she said with a smile that faded when she saw his expression. 'What's wrong?'

'I have something for you.'

'Okay.' Confusion lined every feature of her beautiful face, but there was trust in her eyes. He hoped he would never betray that trust. 'Aaron?' she asked quietly after a moment. 'Are you going to tell me what it is?'

Instead of replying, he stepped back from her and removed the rose petals he'd been keeping in his pocket. It had been a silly idea, he thought now as the confusion intensified on her face. But it was too late to stop now.

He cleared his throat. 'I got these from the house.'

'You stole…petals from the garden?' Her lips curved. 'Just petals? Not the actual flowers?'

He smiled. 'I wanted to take a picture of you standing in a shower of petals.'

'Aaron,' she said after a moment. 'You realise you're being weird, right?'

His smile widened. But he only nodded. She let out a frustrated sigh. 'Okay, fine. Should I just—' She cupped her hands and mimicked throwing the petals into the air.

'Yes. But throw them over your shoulder.' He handed her the petals, careful to protect them from the wind. 'So, turn your back to me while I get the camera ready.'

There was impatience in her eyes now, but she didn't say anything. Only turned her back to him. She was indulging him, he thought. Because that was who she was. Always putting him first, even when she didn't understand why.

He took the ring from his pocket and took another deep breath. And then he got down on one knee and said, 'I'm ready.'

She threw the petals into the sky and turned, a smile on her face for the picture she'd thought he was about to take. At first the confusion returned. Her eyes searched for where she'd thought he'd be as the petals swirled around them. Then, as they were carried up and away by the wind, her gaze lowered, settling on him.

She sucked in her breath and then, on an exhale, said his name. The surprise had turned into something deeper, more meaningful, as she did. And suddenly all the fear, all the uncertainty disappeared.

It was going to be perfect.

That was the last thing he thought before telling her why he wanted to spend the rest of his life with her.

No, he thought as he closed his eyes briefly. There had been no hesitation when Rosa had accepted his proposal.

But hadn't his mother shown him that he would need to take responsibility for others at some time in his life? So why hadn't he realised Rosa might have needed that from him too?

But now that he thought about it, he wondered if it was because he *had* been responsible when it came Rosa. He'd promised her mother that he would look after her. And, since he'd loved her so damn much, marriage had seemed like the perfect way to do it.

But maybe *that* had been his mistake.

Or maybe *he* was the mistake…

'Okay,' he said curtly, ripping himself out of the web his memories had caught him in. 'Do you want another drink?'

She blinked at him, and then silently nodded and handed him her glass. He deliberately brushed his fingers against hers as he took it, and saw the slight shake of her hand as she drew it back to her lap.

He turned away from her, satisfaction pouring through him. Whatever it was that she was going through—whatever it was that *they* were going through—he hadn't made up their attraction. And that attraction had come from their feelings for one another.

Perhaps he'd made one too many mistakes with Rosa. Heaven knew he had with his mother, so it might not have been different with his wife. But at least he could make sure Rosa didn't forget that they were drawn to one another. Something neither of them had ever been able to deny.

And then what? an inner voice asked as he poured their drinks. Would they just become hyperaware of their attraction, since their feelings were seemingly out of bounds, and then let it fizzle out between them?

There was no way that was happening. And if they acted on it...what would that mean for him? For them? Would she just walk away from him again? Would he just let her go?

An uncomfortable feeling stirred in his stomach and he walked back to her, setting her glass down on the table to avoid any more touching. He had no idea what he wanted to achieve with her. With his marriage. And he'd never thought he would be in the position to have to worry about it.

He'd thought he'd done everything right in his life. He'd looked after a mother who hadn't cared about looking after herself. About looking after him. He'd got a stable job. Succeeded in it. He'd fallen in love—though it had been unplanned—and he'd married.

And still everything had gone wrong.

Though, if he was being honest with himself, perhaps that had started when his mother had been diagnosed with cancer and he'd realised the extent of his mistakes.

Now, the fear that had grown in the past four months pulsed in his chest. Had him facing the fact that everyone in his life who was supposed to love him had left him. His mother. His father. And now Rosa…

He couldn't deny that he was the problem any more.

expanding?

CHAPTER FOUR

'SO, WHAT HAVE you been doing these last four
months?'

Somehow, she managed to keep her tone innocent. As if she wasn't asking because she desperately wanted a glimpse into the life he'd made
without her.

It was veering into dangerous territory, that question, and yet it was the safest thing Rosa could
think to ask. Something mundane. Something that
didn't have anything to do with what they'd been
talking about before.

Feelings. Emotions. Their relationship.

But the expression on his face told her that perhaps the question wasn't as safe as she'd thought.
Still, he answered her.

'Work.'

'Work?' When he didn't offer more, she pressed.
'What about work? New clients?'

'New clients.'

She bit back a sigh. 'And?'

'We're expanding.'

'Oh.'

Expanding? He'd never spoken about the desire to expand before. His law firm was one of the

most prestigious family practices in Gauteng. He had wealthy clientele, made sure his firm helped those in need, and he'd always spoken about how content he'd been. Proud, even. So why was he expanding?

She waited for him to offer an explanation. He didn't. And she didn't have the courage to ask him. Not when she would have known if she'd just *stayed*.

'You?'

Her gaze sprang to his. She hadn't expected him to engage. 'I've been working on a new line. Evening gowns.'

'Like the one you're wearing.'

'Exactly like the one I'm wearing. For women like me.'

His eyes swept over her, heating her body with the faint desire she saw on his face. He was controlling it well, she thought. He never had before. She'd always known when Aaron desired her. It would start with a look in his eyes—much more ardent than what she saw there now—and then he'd say something seductive and follow his words with actions.

She'd loved those times. Loved how unapologetic they had been. How freeing. And since they both had problems with being free—no matter how much she pretended that she didn't—those moments were special.

And now she'd lost them.

'It'll be popular.'

'I hope so.' She paused. 'I did a sample line. I've been promoting it on the website for the past month, and it's got some great feedback. I might even do a showcase.'

'I told you it would be great.'

'You did.'

Neither of them mentioned that for years he'd been telling her that she needed to make clothes for herself. For others like her. But that wasn't why she'd got into fashion. At least, not at first. She loved colours, patterns, prints. She loved how bold they could be, or how understated. She loved the contrast of them—the lines, the shapes.

She hadn't wanted to confine herself when she'd started out. She'd wanted to experiment, to explore, to learn about everything. And, because she had, she now had momentum after being labelled a fresh and exciting young designer. Enough that she could finally design the clothes she wanted to. For women who looked like her. Who were bigger. Who weren't conventionally curvy.

She'd shared all her worries, her fears, her excitement with Aaron. And she wanted nothing more than to tell him about the challenges, the joys she'd had creating this new line now.

But the brokenness between them didn't lend itself to that discussion.

Her heart sank and her eyes slid closed.

How had her *safe* question led to *this*?

* * *

Watching her was going to be the only way he'd figure out what was going on in her head. It was clear she wasn't going to tell him. And, since he hadn't exactly been forthcoming himself, he could hardly ask her what was causing the turmoil on her face.

But he couldn't be forthcoming. How was he supposed to tell her that his expansion plans had started the moment his mother had informed him of where Rosa was? He hadn't been interested in finding her…at least, that was what he'd told himself. But then he'd received Liana's email telling him Rosa was in Cape Town.

And suddenly he was planning to expand his firm to Cape Town.

How was he supposed to tell her all that?

'Oh, look,' she said softly, her gaze shifting to behind him. The pain had subsided from her face—had been replaced by wonder—tempting him to keep looking at her.

Dutifully—though reluctantly—he followed her gaze and saw that she was watching the rain. He didn't know what she found so fascinating about it. Sure, it was coming down hard, fast and every now and then a flash of lightning would streak through it. But still, it looked like rain to him. Regular old rain.

And yet when he looked back to Rosa's face he

could have sworn she had just seen the first real unicorn.

She got up and walked in her beautiful gown to the glass doors, laying a hand on them as though somehow that would allow her to touch the rain. It was surprisingly tender, but he refuted that description almost immediately. What he was witnessing wasn't *tender*. How could his wife watching the rain be tender?

But he couldn't get the word out of his mind as she spent a few more minutes there. Then she walked to the light switch in the kitchen and turned it off. The entire room went dark and she murmured, 'Just for a moment,' before returning to her place at the door.

He still wasn't sure what was so special about it. About watching the rain in the dark. But her reaction had cast a spell around him. And now he was walking towards her, stopping next to her and watching the rain pour from the sky in torrents.

'I don't think I've ever seen a storm more beautiful,' she said softly from beside him.

'An exaggeration,' he commented with a half-smile.

She laughed. Looked up at him with twinkling eyes. 'Of course it is. But I like to think that I use my opportunities to exaggerate for effect. Is it working?' she asked with a wink.

His smile widened and, though his heart was still broken from her leaving, and his mind was still lapping up every piece of information she'd given as to why, as they looked at each other, he was caught by her.

He told himself it was the part of him that wanted things to go back to the way they'd been before. The part that mourned because it was no longer an option. Not with how things had shifted between them. Not when that shift had confirmed that they were no longer the same people they'd been before she'd left.

And still he was caught by her.

By her brown eyes, and the twinkle that was slowly turning into something else as the seconds ticked by. By the angles of her face—some soft, some sharp, all beautiful.

He didn't know why he still felt so drawn to the woman beside him when she wasn't the woman he'd fallen in love with any more. Or was it himself he didn't recognise? He'd spent the four months since she'd left racking his brain for answers about what had gone wrong. And what he'd come up with had forced him to see himself in a new light. A dim one that made him prickly because it spoke of things he'd ignored for most of his life.

'Why do you still make me feel like this?'

He hadn't realised he'd spoken until her eyes widened. His gaze dipped to her mouth as she sucked her bottom lip between her teeth. It instantly had his body responding, and he took a step towards her—

And then suddenly there was a blast of cold air on him and Rosa was on the balcony in the rain.

'Rosa! What are you doing?'

But she turned her back to him and was now opening her palms to the rain, spreading her fingers as though she wanted to catch the drops, but at the same time wanted them to fall through her fingers.

'Rosa!' he said again when she didn't answer him. But it was no use. She didn't give any indication that she'd heard him.

He cursed and then took off his shoes and stepped out onto the balcony with her, hissing out his breath when the ice-cold drops immediately drenched his skin.

Her eyes fluttered open when he stopped next to her, and he clearly saw the shock in them. 'What are you *doing*?'

'The same thing as you, apparently,' he said through clenched teeth. 'Care to explain why we're out getting soaked in the rain?'

'I didn't think you'd—' She broke off, the expression on her face frustratingly appealing. Damn it. How was that possible when their lives were such a mess?

'Rosa,' he growled.

'I wanted to get out of that room,' she said. 'I wanted to breathe in proper fresh air and not the stifling air in *that* room.'

'That room is over one hundred and fifty square metres.'

'You know that's not what I meant,' she snapped. 'I just felt…trapped. With you. In there.'

'You felt trapped with me,' he repeated.

'No, not like that,' she said. 'I felt… It's just that room. And the fact that resisting you—resisting us—is so *hard*. Everything between us is suddenly so hard.' She let out a sound that sounded suspiciously like a sob. 'Mostly I feel trapped by what I did to us.' She closed her eyes and when she opened them again he felt the pain there as acutely as if it were in his own body. 'I threw what we had away.'

He took a step forward, the desire to take her into his arms, to comfort her compelling him. But then he stopped and told himself that he couldn't comfort her when he didn't know why. That he couldn't comfort her when, by all rights, she was supposed to be comforting him.

She'd left *him* behind. She'd hurt *him*.

And yet there he was, outside, soaking wet in the rain because of *her*.

He moved back. Ignored the flash of hurt in her eyes.

'We're going to get sick if we stay out here,' he said after a moment.

'So go back inside,' she mumbled miserably.

It was a stark reminder that she hadn't asked him to come outside in the rain with her. And it would be logical to listen to her and go back inside.

Instead, he sighed and held his ground. Tried to commit the experience to memory. He suspected that some day he'd want—no, *need*—to remember this moment, however nonsensical it appeared to be.

To remember how she looked with her curls weighed down by the rainwater, the make-up she wore smudged dramatically on her face. How her one-of-a-kind dress clung to her beautiful body, reminding him of all that he'd had.

To remember how this—standing on a balcony while it poured with rain—spoke of her spirit. The passion, the spontaneity. How he'd never consider doing something like this and yet somehow he found it endearing.

Heaven only knew why he wanted to remember it. Because the feelings that accompanied it *gutted* him. The longing, the regret. The disappointment. Heaven only knew why he was thinking about how incredibly beautiful she was when empirical evidence should have made him think otherwise.

'Why are you looking at me like that?' she demanded.

The misery, the pain in her voice had disappeared. Had been replaced with the passion he was used to.

'Like what?'

'Like *that*,' she told him, without giving any more indication of what she meant. 'You know what you're doing.'

Was he that obvious? 'I'm waiting for you to decide to go inside.'

She stepped closer to him. 'No, you weren't.'

'You'll get sick.'

'And you won't?' He lifted his shoulders in response. She took another step forward. 'You're not helping me feel any less trapped than I already do, Aaron.'

Again, he shrugged. Again, she took a step forward.

'And you're not as unaffected by all this as you're pretending.'

'What are you doing?' he asked, clasping her wrist just before her hand reached his face. Somehow, she'd closed the distance between them as she'd said her last words without him noticing.

'I'm trying to show you that you're not as aloof as you believe,' she said, and dropped her hand with a triumphant smile. 'I told you.'

He didn't reply. He couldn't do so without telling her that she was right—unaffected was the *last* thing he felt. But he showed her. Slid an arm around her waist and hauled her against him.

'Maybe you're right,' he said, his voice slightly breathless, though measured, he thought. But he could be wrong. Hell, he could have been imitating the President of South Africa right then and he wouldn't have known. 'Maybe I was thinking about the first time we kissed.' He dipped his head lower. 'You remember.'

It wasn't a question. And the way her breath

quickened—the way her hand shook as she wiped the rain from her brow—confirmed it.

'Aaron, wait!'

He turned back just in time to see Rosa running towards him. His stomach flipped as it always did when he saw her. And he steeled himself against it. He couldn't fall into the attraction. He hadn't for the last year. He could survive whatever she was running to tell him.

'Would you give me a lift home?' she asked breathlessly when she reached him. As she asked—as he nodded—a menacing boom sounded in the sky before rain began pouring down on them.

'Here, get in,' he said, starting towards the passenger's side of the car. But she put a hand on his chest before he could make any progress, and he held his breath.

Control. Steel.

'No,' she replied tiredly. She leaned back against his car, dropping her hand and lifting her head to the sky. 'No, this is exactly what I need.'

'To be drenched in rain?'

She laughed huskily and need pierced him. 'No. Just…a break.'

'Hard day?'

'Isn't every day?'

She glanced back at the hospital where her mother was staying overnight. His mother had a chemo session but she'd left the book she'd wanted to read at home. And since Rosa's mother—Liana's usual companion—had started a new course of treatment, she wasn't in Liana's session to keep her company.

And because Liana knew Aaron would do anything to make what she was going through easier, she'd asked him to fetch her book.

'But today was particularly hard,' Rosa continued with a sigh. 'I had to meet a deadline for a couple of designs. And my creativity hasn't exactly been flowing over the last few months.'

'I'm sorry.'

'It's okay.' She smiled at him, and then something shifted. He didn't know what it was, but he felt it. It had need vibrating through him again.

'We should go,' he said hoarsely, clenching a fist to keep from touching her.

'What if I'm not ready to go?'

'I'll wait until you are.'

Now, he saw the change. Her eyes darkened. Her lips parted. And he realised how his words had sounded.

'Rosa—'

'No, Aaron,' she said softly, taking a step closer. 'I don't want to—' She broke off. Shook her head. And when her gaze rested on him again, he saw heat there. 'I'm too tired to keep myself from wanting this.'

In two quick movements she gripped the front of his shirt and kissed him.

* * *

'It was outside the hospital,' he continued, the memory and his words weaving the web tighter around them. 'On a rainy day, just like this. You were exhausted after a deadline, but you still came to visit your mother in hospital.' He brushed a thumb over her lips, feeling the shiver the action caused go through them both.

'You asked me to take you home, and for the first time you let me see that you were attracted to me. And then you closed the space between us and told me you were too tired to run from it.'

She was trembling now, though he couldn't tell if it was because of the rain or the memory. It didn't stop him.

'And then you stood on your toes and pressed your lips—'

He stopped when she took an abrupt step back, breaking the spell.

'You're going from "I don't want anything to do with you" to *this*?'

'I wasn't the one who said they didn't want anything to do with the other,' he replied gruffly, forcing himself to take control again. Now, he took a step back and the railing pressed into his back.

'I know that was me. I wanted space. Why won't you give it to me?'

'I didn't plan for us to be locked in together.'

'But you won't even give me a moment to be alone. Why?'

He didn't answer.

'I'm fine out here. Alone,' she said again with a clenched jaw. 'I just wanted some…space. I wanted to feel the rain. I wanted to stop feeling trapped.' She turned away from him, but not before he saw a flash of vulnerability in her eyes. 'You should go inside before we say something to hurt one another even more. '

'So you *are* hurt?'

She shook her head and took another step away from him. Aaron immediately got a strange feeling in his stomach. A familiar feeling. Hollow, sick. The kind of feeling that usually preceded his mother telling him she'd done something stupid. Or him getting the call that confirmed that she had.

Except now he wasn't sure how to understand it. He didn't think Rosa had done something wrong. And if she had he was sure she'd be able to figure it out herself. Unless…

'Are you in trouble?'

'What?' She turned slightly to him. 'No.'

'You don't have to lie to me.'

'I'm not.' But she shifted in a way that made him think that she was. The feeling in his stomach tightened.

'Rosa—'

'Go back inside, Aaron.'

For a moment he considered it. But then he realised he didn't *want* to go back inside. She'd pushed him away before. Then, he didn't have a say in it. If he let her push him away now, he'd be having a say. And he'd be saying that he didn't care about her.

He might not know where they stood with each other, but he *did* know that not caring wasn't the message he wanted to give.

He took a step forward.

CHAPTER FIVE

'Rosa.'

'Go back inside, Aaron.'

'Not until you tell me what's going on with you.'

How many times would she have to tell him that it was nothing? That nothing was wrong? Would she have to keep convincing him? She wasn't sure she could. And her impulsive decision to come outside in the rain was fast becoming one of her worst ones.

She'd just wanted some space, like she'd told him. And she'd wanted to breathe something other than the tension in the air between them.

Now she was sopping wet, the rain finally penetrating her skin. She was cold. She was miserable. And yes, she was in pain. She didn't want things to be the way they were between them. But what choice did she have?

She was doing this for the good of them. She was doing it for *him*. Why couldn't he just leave her alone to do that in peace?

She turned to him now, took in his appearance. He was as soaked as she was, and yet he gave no indication of it. She'd always admired how at home he seemed to be in his body. How he owned the space around it, even though he was taller, stronger, more intimidating than most. He never seemed out of place. Even here, in the rain, soaked to the core, no doubt, he looked as if he belonged.

With me, she thought, and nearly sobbed.

'Let's go back inside then,' she managed quietly, and walked past him before realising she would soak the entire floor if she went in wearing her dress.

The small carpet at the door would probably soak up some of it. But the rest of the floor would not escape unscathed. Forcing herself to be practical, she undid the ties of her dress at her waist. And then she dropped it to the floor before stepping out of it.

She refused to look back. Knew what her actions would seem like, and after what had happened outside…

She was just being practical, she thought again as she turned on the lights and went to the bathroom for towels. When she handed one to Aaron his expression was unreadable.

But the silence between them flirted with the tension that was still there. Wooing it. Courting it. Reminding them of what would have happened at any other time had she stood in front of him in shapewear that clung to the curves of her body.

It was the dress kind that plunged at her breasts and stopped mid-thigh, and hastily she patted down the water from her body before picking up her soaking dress and fleeing to the safety of the bathroom.

She released an unsteady breath when she got there and then squeezed the excess water from her dress, wincing at the destruction it didn't deserve. Making the best of the situation, she hung it over the door and then stepped into the shower. She made quick work of it, knowing that the door was open a smidge now because of the dress. She didn't want to take any more chances with Aaron.

Not that he'd cross that boundary. Not when his control was back in place after what had happened on the balcony. It was stupid to feel disappointed, she admonished herself, and reached for another towel—there seemed to be plenty of them, fortunately—and then tied it around herself before opening the door widely.

And walking right into Aaron.

His hands reached out to steady her, though her own hands had immediately lifted to his chest to steady herself. Only then did she notice that her face was directly in line with his chest. That fact wasn't a surprise. He was significantly taller than her.

No, the surprise was that his chest was bare.

She blinked. Stepped back. And then saw that he wore only the towel she'd given him around his waist.

Her mind went haywire. Memories overwhelmed her. Suddenly she was thinking about all the times she would have jumped into those arms, wrapped her legs around his waist, kissed him. And how those kisses would have turned into something more urgent as soon as she had.

Her breathing went shallow and she told herself to step around him. To ignore how his body hadn't changed. How the contours of his muscles were still as defined, as deep. How his shoulders were still strong, still broad. How his torso was still ripped.

She loved his body. Loved how big and strong he was. How he could pick her up, carry her around and not lose so much as a breath as he did.

Like the time she'd teased him about not wanting to accompany him to some event. He'd threatened to carry her there and, when she'd goaded him, had made good on the threat, though the event hadn't been for hours.

He'd picked her up and tossed her over his shoulder. She'd complained, squirmed, called him a caveman for doing it. But she'd loved it. And when he'd set her down she'd given him a playful punch to the chest before launching herself into his arms and—

'Excuse me.'

His deep voice interrupted the memories and she nodded. Stepped around him. And let out a sigh of relief when some of the tension inside her cooled.

She figured out her clothing options quickly. She'd have to wear the lingerie Liana had packed for her as underwear and, since none of the other clothing would be comfortable, she'd wear one of Aaron's shirts over it.

She was buttoning up the shirt when Aaron emerged from the bathroom, again in nothing but that towel.

Her heart started to thud. She forced herself to focus on something else.

'I'm going to try the kitchen and hope your mother left coffee.' That was something else, she thought gratefully. 'Would you like some?'

He nodded and she walked away as fast as she could. Fortunately, Liana had left coffee and she busied herself with the task. But her mind wandered and, since she didn't want to slip back into memories, she thought about why she'd stepped out into the rain in the first place.

She'd felt claustrophobic. And plagued by the connection she and Aaron had shared. The rain had offered an alternative. An escape. It had seemed like a perfectly logical thing to do at the time. And yet it wasn't.

She'd made too many decisions like that in her life. Because she'd wanted to test herself. To see how those spontaneous decisions made her feel.

It was a form of control, she thought. The only kind she'd had. She'd been lost in the world of her mother's anxiety for the longest time, and those spontaneous decisions had been a reprieve. Even though some of them had been stupid. Even though some of them had got her into trouble. They were *her* decisions. And when she made them, for the briefest of moments she felt free.

But freedom had come at a price. And that price had been—when she'd felt that lump in her breast in the shower—leaving her husband.

Because that lump had made her think she had cancer. And how could she put Aaron through that again when she didn't think he'd fully recovered from his mother's illness? Especially when hers could have been prevented if she'd just made the right decision when she'd had the chance.

But, like so many other moments in her life, she didn't know what the right decision would be. Uncertainty clouded every one she'd made. Even running away to protect Aaron seemed uncertain. And now, as she thought about it, her stomach turned, her heart thudded at the doubt...

'It always used to drive me crazy, how quiet you were,' she heard herself say suddenly. She closed her eyes, told herself it would be better to speak—even if she was speaking about things she should leave in the past—than to let her mind go down that path again.

'I know.'

She whirled around, then shook her head. 'You always know.'

He was wearing jeans and a shirt, though somehow he looked just as gorgeous as he had in his suit. Perhaps because he hadn't buttoned the shirt up entirely, and she could see his collarbone, the start of his chest...

'Not always,' he responded quietly. 'But this, you told me. Too many times to count.'

He walked to the couch, sank down on it with a fatigue she'd rarely seen him show. Her fault, she thought. And added the guilt to the sky-high pile she already had when it came to him.

She sighed. 'You should have told me to stop harassing you.'

'You weren't harassing me.'

She set his coffee on the table and took a seat on a different couch. 'It didn't bother you?'

'How could it? You said it to me before we got together. I can't fault you for something I knew about when we met.'

It was ridiculous to feel tears prick at her eyes, and she took a gulp from her coffee—burning her tongue in the process—to hide it from him. But she'd been reminded of how unselfishly Aaron had loved her.

He wasn't like her father. He would have accepted her anxiety about her health. He would have supported her decision not to get screened for breast cancer. He wouldn't have given up on their relationship, like her father had on his marriage. But she couldn't be sure.

She'd often asked herself why her mother hadn't left her father because of his lack of support. The only answer she had come up with was that her mother had been scared. And that that fear had been rooted in selfishness. Violet hadn't wanted to go through her illness alone. And her marriage— even the illusion of it—prevented that.

But Aaron didn't deserve that. Again, Rosa thought that it would have been selfish for her to stay. To do what her mother had done. And it would have been worse for Aaron because he wouldn't check out like her father had. Worse still because he'd already been through so much.

The decision seemed clear now, though she knew it wasn't. Not when she looked into his eyes. Not when she saw the pain there.

'I didn't mean to drive you crazy.' Aaron spoke so softly Rosa almost thought she'd imagined it.

'I loved it,' she said immediately. 'Not in that moment, of course, because your quietness would always make me run my mouth off about something.' *Like now.* She stared down into her cup. 'But I loved it.'

'But…it annoyed you.'

'No. Driving me crazy and annoying me are two different things. You being okay with things being quiet between us? That drove me crazy. You taking my car to work without telling me? *That* was annoying.'

His lips curved. 'It was more economical.'

'Sure, Mr Big-Shot Lawyer.' She rolled her eyes. 'You were thinking about being *economical*.'

'I was.'

'No, what you were thinking was that my car would help make some of your clients feel more comfortable. Which, after I got through my annoyance at finding myself with your massive SUV when I had to go into town where the parking spaces are minuscule, I'd forgive you for.'

'You always did forgive quickly.'

'Not always,' she said softly.

'Rosa?' She looked up. 'What did I do? What couldn't you forgive?'

CHAPTER SIX

'It wasn't you,' she replied after the longest time. Her heart ached at the look on his face.

'You keep saying that, but how can I believe you?'

'Because it's true.' She set her cup on the table and went to sit next to him, drawing his hands into her own. 'It wasn't you. It was—' She broke off, closed her eyes. Could she tell him she couldn't forgive herself? 'It was me. It *is* me.'

'No,' he said. 'No, it's not. It has to be me. It's always me.'

She opened her mouth as he pulled his hands from hers and stood, staring at him. But no words came out.

'Wh…what do you mean?' she said when she managed to get over her surprise.

'Nothing.'

'No,' she said standing. 'That definitely meant something. What are you talking about, Aaron?'

When she joined him in front of the glass door— just as they'd stood earlier, watching the rain—she felt his entire body tense. She lifted a hand to comfort him, then dropped it, hating how uncertain things had become between them.

He didn't answer her question but she had to make him see that it hadn't been him. And the words spilled from her mouth before she could stop them.

'I found a lump in my breast.'

Aaron immediately snapped out of his self-indulgent moodiness. 'What? When? Are you okay?'

'Yes. I'm fine.' But she crossed her arms over her breasts, her hands on her shoulders. Her self-protective stance. 'It was just over four months ago.'

'Before you left?' She nodded. 'Why didn't you tell me?'

Her eyes lifted to his, but he didn't know what he saw there. It killed him. Just as he feared his lack of oxygen would if he didn't catch his breath soon.

'Because it turned out to be nothing.'

That wasn't the reason, but he let it slide. It was more information than he'd thought he'd get. And when finally he'd caught his breath he asked, 'What was it?'

'A milk duct.'

He lifted his eyebrows as the air swept out of his lungs again. 'A milk duct?' he rasped. 'As in—'

'No! No,' she said with a shake of her head. 'Not a baby, no. It was just something that happened. Hormonal.'

He nodded. Tried to figure out why he felt so... disappointed. Was it because she wasn't pregnant?

Or because she'd gone through this hellish ordeal and hadn't told him about it?

'You should have said something.' He left his spot at the door and headed for the drink he hadn't finished earlier. He downed it, ignoring his coffee.

'I didn't want to worry you.'

He turned around. 'Were *you* worried?'

Confusion spread across her features. 'Yes.'

'Then you should have told me. When you're worried, I should be worried too. That was the marriage *I* signed up for.'

'Yes, but sharing my concerns about—' she threw her hands up '—my career isn't the same as sharing my concerns about my health.'

'Why not?'

'I don't know. This is more important.'

'And you didn't want to share something important with me?'

'No, Aaron, come on. I didn't mean it like that.'

'How did you mean it?' She didn't answer him and he nodded. 'Maybe it's better if you and I just don't talk and get some sleep. You can take the bed. I'll take the couch.'

He spread the throw that hung over the couch over it. Not because he wanted to sleep there— he almost laughed aloud at the prospect of sleeping when things were like this between them—but because he wanted her to realise he didn't want to talk any more.

Everything she'd said tore his broken heart into

more pieces. He could almost feel the shredded parts floating around in his chest, reminding him that he hadn't done enough in their marriage. That he hadn't managed to get her to trust him. To tell him about the *important* things.

She sighed and then switched off the lights again. Moments later, he heard her settle on the bed and he settled on the couch himself. His body barely fitted, but he wouldn't take the bed if she was there. It gave him some sort of sick satisfaction that she'd be aware of his discomfort.

Or was that sick feeling a result of what she'd just told him?

He'd been there when his mother had found her lump—had stayed with her right until the moment they'd told her she was in remission—and he knew what havoc it wreaked.

Granted, his mother wasn't entirely the best example of responding to anything with grace. He knew Rosa would be. Or perhaps not, since she hadn't told him about it. Since she'd run.

Still, he wished he could have helped her through it. After what her mother had gone through—after it had led to her death—he could only imagine how terrified she'd been.

And yet she hadn't told him.

No matter what Rosa said, he knew that had something to do with him. His mother had blamed him for everything since his birth. The fact that things hadn't worked out with his father. The fact that his father had walked away from them…

Never mind that he'd never even met the man who'd supposedly left his mother because of *him*.

'I can hear you thinking,' Rosa called over to him. It had been something she'd say to him in bed often, right before they went to sleep. Except then, she'd turn over and force him to talk about it. And he would, because he'd wanted to share it with her.

Now, he didn't.

'You're not going to say anything, are you?' she said a bit softer, though he still heard her. 'I'm sorry, Aaron. I didn't mean to hurt your feelings. It's just… You know my parents didn't have the most conventional relationship. They didn't share things with one another.'

'We weren't like that,' he heard himself say.

'I know we weren't. But that's because—' he heard rustling, and assumed that she was now sitting up '—we weren't like them.'

'Now we are?'

'Now…things have changed.'

'Because you found a lump in your breast.'

'Yes.' Silence followed her words, but he waited. 'You already went through all that with your mother. I didn't want you to have to go through that with me too.'

He frowned, and then sat up. His eyes had adjusted to the dark and he could see the silhouette of her on the bed. She was sitting up, like he'd thought, and had drawn her legs to her chest, her arms around them, her head resting on her knees. He'd found her like that before. Once, when her mother had just died. And again on each anniversary of her mother's death.

He still couldn't resist it. Even though, as he walked to her, as he sat down next to her on the bed, he told himself he needed to.

'I can't imagine how scared you must have been,' he said softly. 'I wish you'd told me.'

'But—'

'I know you didn't want me to worry. And now I know that you were also thinking about what happened with my mother. But you shouldn't have. You should have thought of us first. Of yourself too.' He paused, struggling to figure out how to tell her what he'd thought she already knew. 'We're... stronger together. No matter what we face, we're stronger facing it together.'

'You don't mean that.'

'I do. Why is that so hard for you to believe?'

'Because I was you, Aaron. And I didn't feel the way you claim to feel now.'

'What do you mean?' Aaron asked her in that quiet, steady way he had. And since his quiet, steady presence had already calmed her, she answered him.

'I didn't ask to be my mother's emotional support when she got sick.' She stopped and wondered if he'd know what she meant by that. That she was talking about her mother's mental illness *and* her cancer.

But her mother's mental illness wasn't a subject she'd ever wanted to talk about—it had been too difficult—though she had mentioned it to him once. But could she expect him to remember something she'd only mentioned once?

She shook the doubt away. 'But I had no choice. My father…was useless with that kind of thing—' *with everything that she'd gone through* '—and my brothers used excuse after excuse to keep from dealing with my mother's illness. Or emotions. Or anything beyond their own lives.' She rolled her eyes at that, much like she had to their faces. 'I was forced into being her carer, and I didn't want to do that to you.'

'I took my vows seriously.'

'But you don't know how… You don't know until you know.'

His hand engulfed hers. 'I do know,' he told her. 'I made those vows intentionally. I'd be there for you in sickness and in health.'

'My parents made those vows too,' she responded quietly. 'And look where that got them.'

'They weren't us.'

'It's not that simple.'

He didn't reply. Only drew her into his arms and slid down so that they were lying together on the bed.

She didn't want this. She didn't want to be reminded of how good it felt to share her worries with
him. How good it felt to lie there in his strong arms
and let him take that burden from her.

But she stayed there and, for the first time in
months, felt herself relax.

CHAPTER SEVEN

THE RAIN HAD calmed slightly when Aaron opened his eyes. It was barely light, and it took him a moment to figure out that he'd fallen asleep. Rosa stirred against him, reminding him of how *she'd* fallen asleep first the night before.

He hadn't had the heart to move her then, and now, though he knew he should, he didn't move. She was still sleeping, but it wouldn't be long before she woke up. It was her habit to wake as the sun came up. She'd check to see if he was still in bed with her. If he was, she'd snuggle against him and go back to sleep. If he wasn't, she'd go find him. Miserable, sleepy, she'd creep into his lap, complaining that if he hadn't been working she'd have been able to sleep longer.

It had been one of her endearing qualities. Much like the fact that she couldn't deal with quiet—his preferred state—so she'd keep talking until he'd answer her.

Things had been good between them. But he could see the cracks clearly now. Her running instead of turning to him when she'd found that lump had been the first sign of it. The last four months—and the last twelve hours—had highlighted the others.

All of which seemed to lead to the same conclusion: she didn't want *them*. She didn't want *him*.

He got up, the thought making him too anxious to continue lying still beside her. He'd never given much thought to being unwanted, though his mother had reminded him of it often enough that he should have.

There were days when she'd told him he was a surprise. Others when she'd call him an accident. It was only when she was feeling terrible about herself that she'd call him a mistake.

But he'd brushed it off. It had been easy to do when he'd been raised by his nanny—a kind woman who his mother's rich family had been able to afford. So the idiosyncrasies of the woman who'd showed up twice a day to say good morning and goodnight to him hadn't really mattered.

And since he'd never met his father, he hadn't cared about that either. His needs had been taken care of. His nanny had been there when he was younger. His mother had become more of a permanent fixture in his life when he got older. And when she'd got sick it had jolted him into realising she was the only family he had.

He hadn't needed anything else until he'd met Rosa. Until he'd married her. Until she'd left. And he'd realised how, despite believing otherwise, being unwanted had affected him.

He went about his morning routine as usual. His mother had thought of practicalities like toothbrushes and toothpaste, fortunately—hell, he'd take what he could at this point—and when he was done he went to the kitchen to make coffee.

'Coffee?' he asked when he heard a rustling behind him.

He made another cup after her sleepy, 'Yes, please,' and by the time he was done she'd emerged from the bathroom looking adorably mussed from sleep.

The shirt she wore was creased, her hair piled on the top of her head. It took less than a minute for his body to react to how much of her legs the shirt now revealed.

He took a steadying breath as he set her cup on the table and then moved to watch the rain through the glass doors. It was easier to do that than to watch her. Than to want her.

Than to need her.

'It's better today,' she said softly from behind him. He grunted in response. The annoyance of the situation was catching up with him now.

Sure, that's it, a voice in his head mocked him.

'We're back to this now, are we?' she said after another few moments of silence. He took a sip of his coffee in response. Pretended not to hear her frustrated sigh.

'Aaron—'

'I'm sorry that you had to go through what you did,' he said, turning to her. 'I'm sorry that you felt you couldn't share that with me. Whatever your reasons were,' he added. 'But clearly we have different opinions on this relationship. Now mine is finally catching up to yours.'

Being locked in that room was torture.

She'd thought it before, when she hadn't alienated her only company. Well, she considered, at least not to the extent that she'd alienated him now. And she wasn't even sure how she'd done it. They'd been on okay terms when she'd fallen asleep. Then, when she'd woken up, she'd found Aaron as aloof as always.

Except he hadn't really ever been aloof with her. With other people, yes. But her? No. Being the recipient of it made her heart ache.

And now she'd also have to live with the silence she'd complained about earlier. For an indefinite amount of time. Within the first hour she was antsy. And then antsy turned into bored. She was desperate to run out in the rain again. But she didn't. Because she was a mature, responsible adult who wouldn't deal with her feelings by doing something that stupid. Again.

Instead, she went to the bed since Aaron had claimed the couch. The bedding was rumpled, the indentation of their bodies still there...

'We have to leave this room at some point,' Rosa said, snuggling into the warmth of Aaron's body. He made a non-committal noise, tightening his arm around her, his free hand lightly trailing up and down her arm. 'We're on honeymoon. We should be going to the beach. Exploring the town. Showing off our love to the world.' He didn't reply. She sighed. 'Fine. For food then, at the very least.'

'We don't need food.'

'Really?' she replied dryly. 'You don't think we're going to need fuel if we want to stay here?'

The side of his mouth lifted. 'I suppose you have a good point there.'

'I know,' she said with a laugh. 'Honestly, I'm not sure how we've survived so long without it.'

He looked down at her, his eyes alight with desire and amusement. 'Probably like this.'

His lips were on hers before she could stop him. And then so was his body, the weight of it a comforting and intoxicating pressure on her aching skin.

Suddenly, all thought of food fled from her mind. Suddenly, she didn't want to stop…

She sucked in her breath at the memory. Brief as it had been, it had stung. It had reminded her of the good times she and Aaron had shared. Not only in their marriage in general, but there, in the very room they were trapped in. On the very bed she was looking at.

And she'd given up on that. On them. Because she'd made the wrong decision a long time ago.

Because, even now, she didn't know how to make the right one.

Desperate to escape from her thoughts, she began searching through the drawers of the bedside tables, hoping to find paper so she could work on a design that would keep her mind busy.

But, almost as quickly as she'd been swept into that memory of her and Aaron, she was drawn into another memory. This time, though, instead of paper she'd found a picture of her mother, holding the flowers they'd both been named after, smiling up at the camera.

The air left her lungs and her legs crumbled. She sagged down onto the bed.

'Rosa?'

His voice was behind her. She hadn't realised he was so close. The bed dipped next to her. His hand covered the one she'd let fall to her lap.

'I didn't realise your mom had this picture,' she said absently. 'It's the one I put next to my mom's hospital bed. A reminder of the flowers we'd been named for. Forces of nature. Symbols of life.'

She smiled. 'I forgot this picture existed.' She traced her mother's smiling face with a finger. 'She looked so happy here. She was pregnant with me, so it was before she got sick.'

'Long before the cancer.'

'No, I meant the hypochondria.' She set the picture on top of the bedside table. Tilted her head as she looked at it. It had been a long time since she'd seen that smile on her mother's face.

'Your mom was a hypochondriac?'

His question lulled her out of the memories, and she quickly realised what she'd told him.

'Yes,' she forced herself to say lightly, and got up. Away from him. 'I told you that.'

'I'm sure I would have remembered if you had.'

'I told you at the funeral.' Her stomach cramped. 'You asked me why people kept telling me how sorry they were that this had actually become something.'

He swore softly. 'I forgot about it.'

'I know.'

'You didn't remind me either. I don't think you've ever spoken about it.'

'No,' she replied with a thin smile. 'I didn't.'

She walked away, towards the door that showed the light shower that was coming down now. She wanted to escape, but it wasn't from the room any more. Or from him. It was from the memories.

From the reminder of how often she'd held her breath, waiting for her mother to tell her how the rash she'd got from being out in the sun was skin cancer. Or how her headaches were a brain tumour.

Rosa's life had revolved around her mother's anxiety. And that anxiety had spilled over into her own life. Rosa had never been free to do what she wanted to, too afraid that her mother would need her.

It had been easier not to make plans. She'd told herself that, and yet she'd still wanted to do things. And the tension between wanting and telling herself that she shouldn't, that she couldn't, had constantly churned in her stomach.

So she'd done spontaneous things. Things she'd wanted to do. She'd chosen to seize the moment because she hadn't known when those moments would be snatched away from her.

And they would inevitably be snatched from her. And she'd mourn the loss of her freedom even as she'd wondered whether she should have done those things in the first place.

'It hurt you.'

The quiet words said from behind her had tears prickling in her eyes. 'It doesn't matter,' she said. Except that it came out in a whisper, which didn't make it sound like it didn't matter. 'It's over now.'

He moved next to her and she thought about how often they'd stood there, like that, since they'd arrived.

'What was it like?'

She shook her head, fully intending not to answer that question. Which was why, when the words came spilling out of her mouth, it was so surprising.

'Difficult. My mother had always been anxious. But it was okay, for the most part, because she could deal with it.' She paused. 'I don't know what changed that. I don't know why she suddenly started obsessing about her health. But by then I'd had already taken on the role of soother. I don't have any memory that wasn't somehow affected by it.'

She blew out a breath. 'People use that term so easily. Hypochondriac. I remember a friend of mine calling a colleague a hypochondriac because she'd take sick leave often. And I found myself asking her whether she knew what that really meant.'

She stepped away from the door now, and began pacing. 'It was terrible, and I felt so bad afterwards. Because her explanation was so pathetic, and didn't come close to what it's really like. How the person can feel themselves suffering. Or how they can see themselves dying. The panic, the anxiety. How they can never truly believe that things are going to be okay. How they can't fully enjoy life because one day they believe life is going to destroy them.'

She didn't mention what it was like for the people around the hypochondriac. How they'd constantly be waiting for the anxiety, for the panic to come. How that would make *them* anxious and panicked. How they'd doubt themselves. Had they handled it properly? Had they done the right thing to help? Had they helped at all?

How, even after the person was gone, they'd still feel the effects of it.

She stopped when her legs went weak and bent

over, waiting for it to get better. And when it did she stood, and saw the conflicting emotions on Aaron's face. He wanted to help her and yet he didn't know if he could.

Her own fault.

'I'm sorry—I didn't mean to go on about it.'

'I asked.'

'I shouldn't have spilled it all out on you like that.'

She walked to the couch, sank down on it.

'You should have,' he said when he took the seat opposite her. 'You should have told me sooner.'

'Apparently there's a lot I should have told you.' She gave him a wry smile. 'And with all my talking too, I hadn't told you any of it.'

'It's part of the reason you left.'

She stiffened, her heart racing. 'What do you mean?'

'There's a reason why, with all your talking, you didn't tell me about your mother. Or open up about it,' he said quietly when she opened her mouth to protest. 'It's probably why you didn't tell me about the lump in your breast either.'

'No,' she denied. But she'd started shaking. He was awfully close to the truth.

'Yes,' he told her. 'You've had to be brave for your mother for so long. You don't know how not to be.'

CHAPTER EIGHT

Rosa released a sharp breath and nodded. 'I suppose you're right.'

And yet, somehow, Aaron felt as if he'd got it wrong. Not entirely, he thought, looking at the pensive expression on her face. But there was relief there too, which made him think that there was something else.

'You should be able to talk with me. Or you should have been able to talk with me,' he corrected himself when that annoying voice in his head reminded him that they were no longer together.

'I've made a lot of mistakes with you,' she admitted softly, and his chest tightened.

'I know. I'm sorry.'

'Why are you apologising?'

'Some of those mistakes were my fault.'

He threaded his fingers together, braced his arms on his thighs, but he refused to drop his head like he wanted to. No, he would face her. He would face the mistakes that he'd made. Especially now, after hearing about her mother's issues.

He hadn't known before. Or, more accurately, he hadn't been paying enough attention. He vaguely remembered her mentioning her mother's hypochondria but, since he'd only ever heard it used in the way she'd described her colleague using it, he hadn't thought much of it until now.

He should have. He should have been more attentive. He should have done his part for her.

'I don't understand how my mistakes could have been your fault.'

'I shouldn't have let you make them.'

Her eyes narrowed. '*Let me?* I don't think that's the correct phrase.'

'I don't mean it that way.'

'Then how *do* you mean it?'

He opened his mouth to explain, and yet every explanation he could think of sounded wrong. And exactly the way she'd thought he'd meant it.

'I was…older than you when we married,' he tried eventually. 'I should have…helped you.'

'Helped me…with what?'

'Helped you see that perhaps marrying me wasn't the best idea.'

Her expression twisted into one that would have been charming had the words he'd just said not turned his heart inside out.

'I…' She blew out a breath. 'No, Aaron. That's not one of the mistakes I was talking about.' She pushed up from her seat now, sat down next to him, curling her legs under her. 'It wasn't a mistake marrying you.' She closed her eyes. 'At least, not for the reasons you mean.'

'But it *was* a mistake.'

She let out a breath again and leaned forward, taking his hand. 'I don't remember ever being happier than that moment you proposed to me. It was like…a light in a terrible darkness that I couldn't get out of. You helped me get out of it.'

'You were grieving for your mother.' He didn't know why he was still speaking. About his fears. About all the things he'd realised since she'd walked into the room. Since she'd left four months ago. 'I should have given you more time.'

'So why didn't you?'

'Because I—'

'What?' she prompted softly when he broke off and didn't continue. 'Because you what?'

'Because I made a promise to your mother to take care of you.' There was a stunned silence, and then her hand left his. He turned to her. 'She didn't ask me to marry you. Just to make sure you'd be okay. It seemed like a natural thing to do because I loved you. And I wanted to live my life in case… Before it was too late.'

She didn't respond. Instead, she shifted back and stared blankly at her hands in her lap.

'Rosa—'

'No—' she cut him off in a hoarse voice '—you just told me one hell of a thing. I need… I need time.'

'Okay.'

He watched helplessly as she stood and began pacing again. He couldn't say more than he had.

Nor could he do anything to make her feel better. So he watched. And waited.

'How do I know?' she asked suddenly. 'How do I know that your proposal wasn't just because of my mother?'

'We'd been dating over a year before I proposed.'

'So what?' She stopped in front of him and rested her hands on her hips. 'So what, Aaron? It was a *year*. Sure, we were friends for a year before that. But what does it matter? We spent most of our time together at the hospital. Can we even call that dating?'

'We got to know each other during that time,' he replied measuredly. 'You got a job designing clothes without any qualifications when you were nineteen. Now you're an incredible success.'

'Because of your mother.'

'My mother might have helped spur it along with her connections, but you got your foot in the door by yourself.'

She clenched her jaw. 'Those are facts. I shared facts with you.'

'I learnt that your drive got you to where you were. And that drive came from a passion to create. That creating calms your mind. That it helps you make sense of things.' Her expression turned softer, and feeling hopeful, he continued. 'I know that your family life was hard. That your father and brothers were hopeless with your mother's disease—and now

I realise how deep that goes—but that it taught you to be strong. Brave.'

'Too brave,' she offered with a smile.

'Only when it comes to trusting the person you agreed to spend the rest of your life with.' Silence pulsed between them, reminding them that they were no longer in that place. But neither of them addressed it. 'Besides, I bought the ring I gave you long before your mother spoke to me.'

Her hands curled into fists, but not before he saw that she was still wearing her ring. He wasn't sure how he'd missed that, but the fact had hope beating in his heart, healing some of the pain there.

'You're lying.'

'I had the ring made the day after you showed me how to dance.'

She stared at him. Shook her head. 'Now I *know* you're lying.'

He smiled. 'I'm not.'

'But that went *terribly*.'

'Only because your instruction ability left much to be desired.'

'*Excuse me?*' she said. 'I'm a *terrific* teacher. The entire reason we were able to do our wedding dance was because of me.'

'You, and the dance instructor I hired to show me how to do the steps after each of our lessons.'

She gasped. 'You did *not*.'

His smile widened. 'I did.'

She stared at him a while longer and then shook her head. 'This is a betrayal.'

'Apparently,' he replied, amused. 'Because you've forgotten the reason I mentioned the dancing in the first place.'

'Firstly—' she lifted a finger '—I taught you to dance out of the goodness of my heart. The reason it went so badly was because you have two left feet. Secondly—' a second finger lifted '—I didn't *want* to teach you our wedding dance. I remembered how badly it went the first time. The only reason I did it was because I didn't want you to look silly when we danced in front of all your fancy colleagues. Though now, of course,' she muttered darkly, 'I wish I'd left you to embarrass yourself. And thirdly—' a third finger lifted, and then she threw both hands in the air '—why on earth would that make you want to marry me?'

He stood now, ignoring the way her eyes widened when he took her hand and put it on his shoulder, before resting one hand on her waist and taking her other hand in his.

'Because,' he said as he started swaying, 'I could smell your perfume when we did. It made me realise I'd be okay if that was the only scent I'd smell for the rest of my life. And having you in my arms made me think that I'd be okay if that was the only thing I could feel for the rest of my life.' He pulled her closer until her body was pressed against his. Something akin to belonging washed over him. 'I also loved how hard you tried to make me think you weren't annoyed with me. And that smile you'd give me every time I'd step on your toes.'

'You're doing pretty great now.'

'That's because I always knew how to dance,' he said with a crooked smile. Felt it widen when she frowned at him.

'But the instructor?'

'Didn't exist.'

'I don't understand.'

'It's simple, really,' he said, and stopped moving. 'I'd lie about anything if it gave me an opportunity to do this.'

He lowered his lips onto hers.

She'd seen it coming. In the way his eyes had first softened, then heated. She could have stopped it. Should have. Instead, she closed her eyes and let herself be swept away by her husband's kiss.

Oh, how she'd missed it. The way his lips knew how to move against hers. The way his tongue knew how to tangle with hers. It sent shivers down her spine just as intensely as it had the first time he'd kissed her. The butterflies were there too, as was a need she hadn't known could exist inside her. As was a want she didn't think would ever go away.

His arms tightened around her. Pulling her in. Keeping her safe. She could feel the strength in them and then in his hands, when they moved from her waist, down over her butt, squeezing gently before coming back up over her hips.

Her body shuddered under his touch. Her breath hitched as he deepened the kiss. As his hands moved up over the sides of her breasts to take her face in his hands. He was being gentle, sweet, and she would have protested against it—against the control she knew it required from him—if she wasn't so desperate for the taste of him.

As it was, her hands couldn't stay still. They slid over the grooves of his muscles. His back, his shoulders, his arms. Down between them, over his chest. His abdomen trembled under her touch when her hands lowered, and she felt the effect she had on him press against her stomach.

'Wait,' he said, gently pulling away from her. Which was strange, she thought, a bit dazed, since the expression on his face was fierce, obviously pained, and far from gentle. 'I can't do this with you.'

'Do what?'

'This.' His hands tightened slightly on her arms and then he took a step back. Controlled, she thought again, and a violent wave of resentment washed over her.

'You were the one who started this, Aaron,' she said in a low voice.

'It was…a mistake.'

He walked away from her and the pain that

spasmed in her chest was so intense she thought her heart had broken.

'I'll add it to the list, I suppose.'

'Another thing that's my fault.'

'Oh, stop that,' she snapped. Hurt and anger had done dangerous things to her patience. 'Nothing that happened between us is your fault. I married you because I wanted to. I left you because I had to. That's it. End of story. I'm not your mother, Aaron. You don't have to take responsibility for me. Or for something that you didn't cause.'

CHAPTER NINE

'IT'S NOT THE SAME.'

'Isn't it?' she shot back. 'Because that's what I'm hearing right now.'

Aaron couldn't describe the emotions going through him. It was a mixture of desire and annoyance. Anger and frustration. All because of her. He shook his head.

'I'm not going to have this conversation with you.'

'What else are you going to do?' she exclaimed. 'Walk out through the locked door?'

'It won't be locked for long,' he said, and made the kind of spur-of-the-moment decision he'd warned himself against. He walked to the door and then took a couple of steps back. Enough so he could plough through it.

'Aaron?' There was panic in her voice. 'What are you doing? Aaron,' she said again when he didn't answer. When he began to move forward, she shouted, 'No!'

It wasn't that she'd shouted at him. It was more the complete panic in her tone that stopped him. A few seconds later, she was standing in front of the door, her back against it, arms spread out, shielding the door with her body.

'Are you out of your mind?' she said in a shaky voice. 'You can't break down this door.'

'Why not?'

'What would happen if it didn't work?' she demanded. 'You would no doubt hurt yourself, and there's absolutely nothing in here that would help me look after you.' Her chest was heaving. 'I wouldn't be able to call for an ambulance, and who knows how long it'll be until we get out of here?'

'Careful,' he said quietly. Dangerously. 'You almost sound like you care.'

'I *do* care,' she said through clenched teeth. 'I wish I didn't, but I do.'

'Then what's the real reason you left?'

'Because I found a lump in my breast. Because I immediately thought I had cancer. Because I remembered a doctor had told me that I should get screened for breast cancer. Because, in some stupid, misguided cling to independence, I decided against it.' She sucked in air. Continued. 'Because I thought about how my life would change while I went through chemotherapy. Because I knew I couldn't put you through that again.' Her voice caught at the end and he cursed himself for forcing her to speak.

'Rosa—'

'I told the doctor that my mother had cancer, that I hadn't been screened for it, and they gave me all the tests. I sat through the whole process fearing the worst and in the end there was nothing. *Nothing.*'

She lifted her hand and let it fall on her last word. 'So I'd insisted, and imagined it all, and there was nothing.' Her eyes shone when she lifted them to his. 'Just like my mother.'

And suddenly Aaron understood why it had affected her so badly. And why she really had left because of the lump. With quick steps he pulled her into his arms and held her as her body shook.

He closed his eyes. Told himself he was an absolute jerk for pushing. And when the shaking subsided he pulled back and saw that her eyes were dry. That it hadn't been tears at all, just…shaking.

'You're not like your mother.'

'You don't know that.'

'I know it just as well as I know that you're not like *my* mother either.'

'And where does that get us?' she asked, pulling away from him now. 'We still have a broken relationship.'

'Because you were scared about having cancer.'

She stared at him and then shook her head sadly. 'No. No, that's not it at all.'

'Tell me then,' he said urgently, an unknown fear compelling his words. 'Tell me what I'm not understanding.'

'I don't want to be in a relationship with anyone, Aaron. That's why I shouldn't have married you. That's why I left.'

* * *

How could she have hurt him more than she already had?

She hadn't thought it possible, and yet here she was, watching the hope on his face transform into something uglier. And then his expression went blank, his calm façade back in place.

She hated it.

'I'll file the divorce papers as soon as I get home.'

'No, Aaron—'

'No, what?' he said almost conversationally. 'You don't want to be divorced? Because that's the reality of our situation, Rosa. You don't want to be in a relationship with anyone. You made that clear four months ago. You've made it clear now.'

'But... I don't want to be divorced either,' she replied lamely.

'You have to make a decision,' he said coldly now. The tone she'd heard him use with opposing council. 'You can't have it both ways. If you want to fix this, we'll make that decision together and try our best to fix it. If you don't, I file for divorce when I get back and we end this. Either or. Not both.'

She bit her lip when he turned away from her, the tears she'd resisted earlier threatening to spill over now.

But a sound at the door distracted her. She took a step back automatically, felt Aaron approach, placing himself between her and the door. Seconds later, a red-faced man was standing in front of them.

'Aaron and Rosa Spencer?'

'Yes,' Aaron answered.

'Sergeant Downing.' He showed them his badge. 'Liana Spencer—your mother?—called to say that there might be some trouble here. Was she right?'

Rosa heard the hesitation in the man's voice and for the first time realised how it must look to him. Aaron was wearing a wrinkled shirt and jeans, barefoot, and she wore only his shirt. It looked less like the captive situation he'd thought he'd be stepping into and more like an invasion of privacy.

'She was right,' Aaron replied. Cool. Collected. Always. Though he'd stepped in front of her, blocking her from the sergeant's view. 'The door was locked. We couldn't get out.'

'Not locked.' Rosa peered from behind Aaron to see the sergeant lift his hand to his chin. 'It was jammed and I had to use some force, but it opened.'

'So…no one locked us in?' Rosa asked softly. Aaron stiffened in front of her.

'No, ma'am.'

'And the electricity?' Aaron asked.

'We're working on it.' Sergeant Downing frowned. 'Your mother told us she was worried about you and to check. She told me about the spare key she left with the security company down the street.' He paused. 'The only reason I knew to check up here—' his face went red '—was because I…er…heard voices.'

Rosa could only imagine what those voices must have sounded like to an outsider.

'Thank you, Sergeant.'

Aaron didn't move from where he stood, didn't offer the hand she knew he would have if he wasn't still protecting her. Her heart swelled, though she wasn't sure how. She was certain it had broken.

'We couldn't contact you, and with the storm… We thought we'd be stuck here all weekend.'

'You're welcome,' Sergeant Downing replied. 'Well, then, the rain's calmed somewhat, but it's still pretty bad out there so I should be off. There's bound to be another emergency somewhere. A missing dog or something.' He winked at them and only then did Rosa noticed the shimmer of raindrops on his coat. 'You two try to stay out of trouble for the next twenty-four hours.'

'Twenty-four?' Rosa spoke again, almost without noticing that she had. 'Will the storm be continuing until tomorrow?'

'That's the expectation, though you know what the weather's like on this side of the world.' He paused. 'I know this is probably a much better place to ride out this weather—and since I'm a police officer I'm supposed to tell you that you should stay inside until it gets better outside—but this weekend is our annual heritage celebration.'

'In winter?'

'Yeah,' Sergeant Downing said with an indulgent smile. 'We don't get many visitors this time of year, and our founders rocked up here on the fifteenth of this month, so we celebrate. It's nothing major— just some food, some wine, some music inside city hall—but we'd love to have you.'

'We won't—'

'Thank you so much, Sergeant Downing,' Rosa spoke over Aaron. Again, she felt him stiffen. 'We appreciate the invitation. And your assistance.'

'It's fine. And, while I'm here, I'll write down my number in case things get rough again.' He took out a notepad and pen and wrote quickly before handing Aaron the paper. 'Things should be up and running again in a few hours at best—by the end of the day at worst—so you should be able to call. Otherwise, I'll see you in the city.'

He nodded at them and a few moments later they were alone.

'I'd better go down and make sure he locks up,' Aaron said.

'Do you want to go?' she asked instead of replying.

'Do I want to go to the heritage celebration?' he asked, and then shook his head. 'I can think of better things to do.'

'Like spend your time here, alone with me?'

His expression grew stony. 'You're more than welcome to go.'

'How?'

'Take my car.'

She lifted her brows. 'So you really won't go with me?'

'Rosa, I've told you where I stand. You're on the side that doesn't allow me to go with you.'

He left the room before she could reply.

She wasn't on the top floor when Aaron returned. Which was fine, he told himself, because he was tired of whatever was happening between them.

He wondered if his mother had given any thought to the havoc her plan would wreak. Liana hadn't known why Rosa had left him—*he* certainly hadn't, so she didn't find out from him, at least. Though now that he knew she'd been in contact with Rosa, perhaps his wife *had* told Liana why she'd left...

He dismissed it almost instantly. His mother would have told him if she'd known what had happened. It would have been an opportunity to tell him where he'd gone wrong, and she'd never be able to resist that.

He couldn't describe his relationship with his mother. Liana had kept him at a distance for most of his life. And then she'd got sick and things had changed between them. Probably because *he'd* been determined to change things between them, and he acknowledged that he'd bridged the gap more than she ever had.

But watching her suffer the way she had... His

stomach turned just thinking of it. It had been enough to ignore the fact that she hadn't wanted the reconciliation as much as he had. It had been enough to move his life to Cape Town until she got better.

Maybe it was time to face the truth—that his mother still didn't want the relationship he'd tried to forge with her. Perhaps, this weekend, she'd wanted him to face the fact that the end of his marriage had been his fault. Or perhaps she'd been trying to fix it. Which, if that was true, would have been ironic since he'd been cleaning up *her* mistakes his entire life.

I'm not your mother, Aaron. You don't have to take responsibility for me. Or for something that you didn't cause.

He sat down heavily on the couch, clutching the glass of rum he'd poured for himself, Rosa's words echoing in his head. Maybe he *was* conflating the two issues. Rosa and his mother were nothing alike. And Rosa was right. She had a mind of her own. And she'd never expected him to clean up after her. She'd always taken responsibility for what she'd done, even if what she'd done had been spur-of-the-moment.

'Aaron?'

When he looked up Rosa was hovering in the doorway, wearing fitted jeans and his shirt, which she'd paired with ankle boots. 'Where'd you get the clothes?'

'I found some things I left behind the last time we were here.' She shifted her weight from one foot to the other. Was she remembering how different things had been the last time they were there? 'The shoes are your mother's.'

'No top?'

Her cheeks turned pink. 'No.'

He frowned at her reaction, but didn't ask her about it.

'I'm going to go into town. Are you—' She broke off, cleared her throat. 'You're sure you don't want to come along?' He shook his head. 'Okay. Right. Fine.' She paused. 'Well, I'll try to find somewhere else to stay then.' Her gaze met his. 'Since there's a line in the sand now.' She stepped back and then nodded. 'Take care of yourself, Aaron. I'll make sure your car gets back to you in one piece.'

And then she was gone. Seconds later he heard the garage door opening and then closing again. He didn't move. Just kept wondering if this really would be the last time he'd see his wife.

If it was, it would be his fault. He'd been the one who'd drawn a line in the sand. Who'd given them sides to stand on. He was the one who'd told her that she needed to decide between saving or ending their marriage.

Really, it had been selfish. Because he'd hoped that his ultimatum would force her into letting him in. She had—a little. She'd told him about her mother's illness, how she'd thought she was becoming like her mother when she'd found that lump.

But it was so obvious that she *wasn't* like her mother.

Why hadn't she believed him?

And what had she meant when she'd said she shouldn't be in a relationship with anyone?

Clearly, she'd been right when she'd told him he didn't get it. He didn't. He didn't understand how she could claim that marrying him had *and* hadn't been a mistake. He didn't know how she could say she didn't blame him and yet not want to be with him.

It was hopelessly messy. He hated it. Hated how much it reflected the messiness of his mother's life.

With a sigh, he went downstairs to try to find the suitcase he'd brought with him when he'd thought he'd be staying at the house for the weekend. He found it in the room he and Rosa had shared when they'd been there last. He ignored the memories that threatened and was on his way to the shower so he could change when he glanced into the closet Rosa had used the last time they'd been there.

She was right. There were extra clothes of hers there. Including three or four long-sleeved tops, any of which she could have worn out that night.

So why had she worn his shirt?

CHAPTER TEN

Rosa pulled in to the city hall's car park with a sigh of relief. Sergeant Downing hadn't been joking when he'd said it was still pretty bad outside. She'd driven forty the entire way, praying that she wouldn't bump into anything since the visibility was so bad.

Which was probably for the best. She didn't want to be reminded of all the things she and Aaron had done together on the island in happier times.

Things hadn't ended particularly well between them now, but she hoped that he'd realise her leaving hadn't been his fault. Though she didn't think that was the case. She'd botched the explanation. Partly because she couldn't say that she was a *hypochondriac*. Not out loud. She could barely think it. The other part was because she didn't think he'd respond well to her saying she'd done it for his own good.

So, really, she'd given him all that she could.

Her fingers shook as she unbuttoned Aaron's shirt. It was pathetic, lying to him about why she was wearing it. Especially since he could so easily figure out that it *was* a lie. But she didn't care.

The shirt would remind her of the last day they'd

spent together. Even if it wasn't exactly his, she could still smell him on it. Remnants of sleeping together the previous night, which proved that he'd held her while they'd slept.

She pulled it off, held it to her chest for a moment, and then folded it neatly and set it on the passenger seat. Then she pulled at the long-sleeved top she'd put on under Aaron's shirt and hurried into the hall, her handbag the only protection she had against the rain.

She worried she'd made a mistake when she walked in and saw only unfamiliar faces, though that feeling in itself was familiar. It had accompanied all of her spur-of-the-moment decisions. And when Sergeant Downing had told her about this event, right after she and Aaron had had such an immense argument, it had seemed like the perfect escape.

And since that was what she did—ran, escaped—she'd come.

She shook the water off her clutch and then walked further into the room as though she belonged.

'Ms Spencer?'

She whirled around, felt a genuine smile on her lips when she saw Sergeant Downing. 'I hope you meant it when you invited me.'

'Of course,' he replied with a smile. He was handsome, she noticed for the first time. He had short curls on his head, dimples on either side of his mouth that became more pronounced when he smiled. If she hadn't been so entirely enthralled by her husband, she might have been interested.

'This place is pretty big for such a small town.'

'Yeah.' He stuffed his hands into his pockets, looked around. 'It's meant to hold the entire town. We're about six thousand, so it has to be pretty big.'

'It's lovely,' she said, taking in the hall.

It was decorated informally, with stands throughout the room that held food and other goodies. A makeshift bar stood against the wall on one side. There was an elevated platform on the other side, where children chased each other and screamed, and parents soothed and chatted in groups.

The windows were high—almost at the roof—and were spattered with rain, though they provided enough light for the room that the fairy lights that had been haphazardly draped throughout weren't entirely necessary.

'You have generators here?'

'Yep.' He lifted his shoulders. 'City hall is also the designated safe venue for disasters.' He gave her a chagrined smile. 'Small town.'

'Oh, no, I love it. Apart, you know, from the fact that I was locked in a room with my husband for a day because we couldn't make any calls.'

He laughed. 'Speaking of your husband…'

'He's not coming,' she said, her body stiffening. 'He's tired, and me being out the house is giving him the chance to…rest.'

He studied her but only nodded. 'Shall we get something to drink?'

Relieved, she said, 'Sure.'

She followed him to the bar but, when she saw that there was a hot drinks stand right next to it, pivoted and ordered a hot chocolate instead of the alcohol she'd first wanted. Sergeant Downing seemed well-liked by the town—certainly well known, though in a town of six thousand that was expected—and when he began to introduce her as 'Ms Spencer' she automatically corrected him.

'It's Rosa,' she said while she took the hand of the elderly woman who'd handed her the drink.

'That's a lovely name,' the elderly woman—Doreen—said.

'Thank you. I was actually named after my mom's favourite flower. It's a tradition in our family. For the daughters, at least.'

'How lovely.' Doreen beamed. 'It's almost like our Charles over here.'

Rosa glanced over just in time to see Sergeant Downing wince. She cocked an eyebrow. *'Charles?'*

'He was named after his mother's favourite royal,' Doreen offered enthusiastically.

Both her eyebrows rose.

'My mother's always been unique,' Sergeant Downing told her grimly. 'Thanks for that, Doreen.'

'It's a pleasure.'

Rosa laughed. 'Thanks for the hot chocolate, Charles.'

'Charlie,' he replied with a smile. 'You're welcome.'

The whole encounter made some of the sadness that inevitably came when she spoke about her mother ease. Which was strange, considering that she barely spoke about her mother outside of her family. Hell, she barely spoke about her mother *in* her family.

Her father and brothers' lives had pretty much gone on as usual after her mother had died. They lived in Mossel Bay, a small town on the Garden Route in the Western Cape. She'd grown up there, and had then gone to Cape Town when she'd started college. And then, when she'd dropped out, she'd started working for a commercial chain as an intern, before working up to a junior and then senior designer, with help from Liana's connections.

She'd only gone home a couple of times since she'd left for college. The first to pick her mother up and take her to Cape Town so that she could help take care of her as she went through her treatment. Her father and brothers would visit once a month, sometimes twice, which was hopelessly too few times, and yet every time she'd told them that they'd told her they had their own lives to live.

And so that had been that. Even after her mother had died, and Rosa had gone home to pack up her mother's things, it had been Aaron who had been by her side, helping her through it all.

Her brothers hadn't been interested. Her older brother had just started his own business and was more interested in Aaron's legal advice than their mother's belongings. And her younger brother had just got married to someone Rosa had only met once, and he'd been no help whatsoever.

And as for her father... Well, he'd been living a life separate from his wife for a long time by then. Now, of course, he was living with the title of 'widower' and enjoying the attention.

No, Rosa thought again. She hadn't been able to talk about her mother in the longest time. She hadn't wanted to bring it up with Aaron because... Well, because she hadn't wanted to remind him of how terrible their experience with cancer had been.

It had been long after his mother had gone into remission and her mother had passed away that Aaron had relaxed. She'd only then realised how negatively he'd been affected by it all. He'd finally started eating properly. He'd smiled more. He wouldn't toss and turn as much at night.

She hadn't wanted him to slip back into the person he'd been before. Hadn't wanted that for herself either. So she'd left. Protected him from going back. And felt *herself* revert as she did. She'd been foolish to believe it was possible for her to do otherwise when her life was still shadowed by what she'd gone through with her mother.

'Rosa?'

She blinked and then offered a smile to Charlie when she saw his questioning look. 'Sorry. It's been a rough morning. What did I miss?'

He gave her a sympathetic look. 'I don't think I'm going to be making your day any easier, I'm afraid.' He hesitated. 'Your husband managed to get hold of me just now. He says he has your phone, and asked whether I could pick it up for you.'

Aaron was waiting at the front door when Sergeant Downing rang the doorbell. There was surprise on the man's face when Aaron opened the door almost immediately after the bell sounded.

'Hi,' the sergeant said cautiously. 'You called.'

'Yes. Thank you for coming.'

'Rosa insisted.'

Aaron paused as he reached for Rosa's phone on the table next to the door. 'You spoke with her?'

The man's face turned a light shade of red. 'Yeah. I was with her when I got the call.'

Now Aaron turned to face the man fully. 'You were with my wife when you got my call,' he repeated.

'Not like that,' Sergeant Downing said quickly. And then he straightened his shoulders. 'I was the one who invited her. Both of you,' he added. 'And when I saw you weren't with her...' He trailed off. 'Well, I didn't want her to feel alone. Like she was amongst strangers.'

'She was. Is.'

'Yes, but she didn't have to be.'

Aaron considered it for all of a minute. 'You're right. I should probably come back with you. I'll give Rosa the phone myself, and make sure that she isn't amongst strangers any more.'

CHAPTER ELEVEN

ROSA SMILED WHEN she saw Charlie walk through the door of the hall, but the smile froze in place when she saw Aaron following closely behind him.

'What is it, dear?' Doreen asked worriedly when she turned back to Rosa with an outstretched hand that Rosa was meant to supply with a cup of hot water.

'Nothing,' she said, and quickly turned to pour the hot water from the dispenser. She cursed quietly when she saw her hand shaking and told herself to stay steady when she turned back to Doreen. 'Sorry about that,' she murmured, and kept her eyes on the woman who was now making tea for a customer.

After Charlie had left, Rosa had wondered around aimlessly until deciding that her mind would be put to better use if she was working. So she'd asked Doreen if she could help, and had been doing so for the last twenty minutes.

But suddenly working with hot liquids didn't seem like such a great idea.

'Charles, you're back,' Doreen exclaimed, and Rosa was forced to look up and into her husband's eyes.

They were steady as they met hers, as if he hadn't an hour ago told her he'd be filing their divorce papers when he got home.

'I didn't realise you were picking up my phone *and* my husband, Charlie,' Rosa said, pleased with how calm she sounded.

'Your husband?' Doreen exclaimed—the woman really only seemed to have one way of speaking. 'I thought you were here with our Charles.'

'No, Doreen,' Charlie interrupted quickly. 'We're not here together. I actually invited Rosa and her husband, Aaron, to come here this evening when I was on a call to their house.'

'Which house is that?'

'The Spencer property off Main.'

'You're Liana Spencer's son?' Doreen asked, her voice raised even higher.

'Yes, ma'am,' Aaron replied with a nod.

'Why, son, let me give you a hug.' Doreen walked around the table and made good on her word. Rosa's lips twitched. Her husband didn't feel comfortable with public displays of affection, let alone displays with *strangers*. It was kind of adorable to watch.

The older woman's head barely reached Aaron's chest and she gave him an unexpectedly tight squeeze. Rosa hadn't imagined the woman's body had had the strength to give it.

'Thank you,' Aaron said when Doreen pulled

back, and Rosa didn't bother trying to hide her smile.

'No, dear, that was me saying thank you to you.' Doreen dug into the front of her apron and pulled out a crumpled tissue which she pressed to her face. 'Your mother let me and my boys—all three of them, and their wives and my seven grandkids— stay in that house for a month after the place we'd all been staying in burnt down.'

'That was the Spencer place?' Charlie asked now, interest alight on his face. 'Yeah, I remember. I'd forgotten about it.'

'We didn't have any money to spend on staying somewhere else, and we lost everything in that fire. The insurance was giving us a hard time—' Doreen cut off, sniffled. 'And then one day, out of the blue while I was talking to someone in the grocery store, your mom came by and told me she'd heard what had happened and that we could stay in her house until we found something else.'

'Where did she go?' Aaron asked after a moment.

'Not sure. She was gone by the time we got there, and she didn't once check in with us.' Doreen pressed the tissue under both eyes before stuffing it back into her apron. 'Of course, that didn't mean we took advantage. I made sure that house stayed spick and span. And that nothing broke, even though all the grandkids are under ten.'

Aaron's eye twitched. 'I appreciate that, ma'am.'

'Your mother is a good woman, boy.' Doreen reached up and patted Aaron's cheek. 'Now, if you want anything from me or my boys, you can have it for free. Make sure they know it's you and that I told you that, and they won't give you any trouble.' She cocked her head. 'They're good boys too.'

The only thing Aaron had wanted to hear less than an old woman telling him she'd thought Sergeant Downing and Rosa were on a date was that his mother was a good person.

'Bet you didn't expect that,' Rosa said when they finally managed to escape the woman. The sergeant had wisely found someone else to engage with.

'No.' He led them to a less populated area in the corner of the hall. 'You seem to be having a good time here.'

'It's been okay.' They took two empty seats and, for the first time, Aaron noticed she wasn't wearing his shirt.

'You've changed your clothes.'

She looked down. Immediately colour spread over her cheeks. 'I…yes.'

'The shirt?'

'Is in the car.'

'I thought you didn't have anything else to wear?'

She shrugged, which would have annoyed him if he hadn't already known that she'd had something else to wear. And maybe that was part of the reason he'd decided to accompany Sergeant

Downing. Because she'd seemed to…want something of him.

Though the tinge of jealousy at Sergeant Downing's words and the panic that had risen with the D-word had contributed to his decision too.

'You know that's technically not my shirt.' She made a non-committal noise. He almost smiled. 'So you stole it for nothing.'

'I didn't steal it.' She looked over at him and something on his face made her roll her eyes. 'You're teasing me.'

'I'm asking.'

'I didn't steal it,' she said again. 'I…kept it. As a memento.'

'Of what?'

'This weekend.'

'It's been terrible.'

She laughed. That sound had always weakened something inside him. And he realised that she hadn't laughed nearly as much as he'd have liked since they'd been on the island.

'You're right,' she answered. 'But… If this was going to be the last time you and I spend any time together, I wanted to remember it.'

'Even if it was terrible?'

'Even if it was terrible.'

'Why?' he asked after a moment.

'Because it hasn't always been terrible,' she replied, surprising him with her answer. 'We were happy.'

'Yeah, we were.'

'The way things ended,' she said suddenly, her eyes meeting his. The emotion there stole his breath. 'It had nothing to do with the way things were, okay?'

'I'm not sure I can believe that.'

'You have to.' She reached out, took his hand. 'I told you. All of it… It's my fault. I'm the reason things ended badly. Me. It has nothing to do with you.'

'You felt like you had to leave.'

'It's not that simple.'

'It is to me.'

He turned his hand over so that their fingers intertwined.

'I know you see things in black and white.' Her gaze was on their hands. 'If something went wrong between us, it's because someone did something wrong. But…that isn't what happened here.'

'Maybe,' he said. 'But you said it was a mistake marrying me.'

'Only because I shouldn't have put you in this position in the first place.'

'This is—was—a marriage, Rosa. You didn't put me in any position. I chose to be here. We both did.'

'But I shouldn't have.' Her words were soft. Insistent. 'You deserve more than this. You deserve more than *me*.'

His grip tightened on hers as surprise fluttered through him. 'That's not true.'

'It is.'

She blinked and stared ahead at the crowds of people, though he didn't think she saw any of them. And suddenly he thought how strange it was that they were sitting here, in the corner of a hall in a small town, surrounded by strangers, having the kind of conciliatory discussion they hadn't been able to have when they'd been alone.

'I might turn out just like her, Aaron.' She said it so softly he thought he'd imagined the words. 'I might turn out to be exactly like my mother.'

'You won't.'

She turned to him, the smile on her lips unbearably sad. 'You don't know that. The cancer scare... it could be the first of many. Or it could lead to actual cancer.'

'Because she had it?'

'Yes.' She paused. 'And because I refused to take the test to screen for it after she died.'

Silence slithered between them. He wanted to break it. To keep the momentum of their conversation—her honesty—going. But his mind was still processing what she'd said. He couldn't think what to say to keep the silence from choking them.

He saw her more clearly now. Understood the extent of the terror she must have gone through. The blame she'd taken on herself. Her cancer scare took on a deeper meaning. Again, he wished he could have been there. Didn't understand why she hadn't turned to him.

'Why did you refuse?'

She lifted her shoulders. 'I'm not sure.'

But he could see that that was a lie. She knew why she hadn't taken that test. She just wasn't ready to talk about it. Pain drenched his heart.

'Did your mother ever see someone about…' He trailed off, unsure of whether she'd answer. But she didn't seem to mind.

'Sometimes. When it got really bad I'd be able to talk her into seeing a psychologist.'

'Did it help?'

'For as long as she went.' She paused. 'But when she got to that point—when she actually decided to go—it had already got so bad that she had no choice but to acknowledge something was wrong.' She wrapped one arm around herself, held her chin up with the other. 'The therapy would help, then she wouldn't experience such intense symptoms for long enough that she could convince herself that she was fine.' Her eyes met his. 'It was a vicious cycle.'

He nodded. 'And you…?'

'Have I seen someone?' She laughed dryly and dropped the hand at her chin. 'No. That would entail admitting something was wrong.' The laughter sobered. 'No, I'm too much like my mother to let that happen.'

'You've already told me,' he reminded her softly.

'Only because I wanted you to know that none of this—' she waved a hand between them '—is because of you. And, trust me, it was hard enough telling you.'

He knew it had been. Which was why it meant so much to him. Even if there were some things she was still keeping from him.

Hope began to bandage some of the pieces of his heart together again. Perhaps foolishly. But his black and white view of things told him that they'd identified the problem. And, since they had, maybe they could find the solution…

'We should probably stop being so antisocial,' he said suddenly.

She blinked. 'What?'

'Let's go talk to your friend.' He stood, held out a hand to help her up.

'My friend—Charlie?' He nodded, and was proud that he managed to keep himself from rolling his eyes. 'Why?'

'Because when I walked in here you looked happy to see him.'

She gave him a strange look, but took his hand and stood. 'You're not going to try and get on his good side and then beat him up, are you?'

He smiled. 'No.' Though that wasn't a bad idea.

'I'm not sure I trust this change in attitude.'

'You should,' he said, serious now. 'You need happy. If happy means you talk to a man and the old woman who believes that the two of you should be together, then that's what we'll do.'

She stared at him and then a smile crinkled her

eyes. It hit him as hard as her laugh had. More, when she reached a hand up to his cheek and stood on her toes to press a kiss to his lips.

'I knew I didn't deserve you,' she said softly, the smile fading. And then she took his hand. 'Come on. Let me introduce you to some new friends.'

CHAPTER TWELVE

Rosa had thought that the term 'new friends' would cause Aaron to give up his appeasing mood and run far, far away.

Except it hadn't. In fact, right at that moment, she was watching him engage in a conversation with Charlie about some legal show they both happened to enjoy.

Of course, for Aaron that meant that he said one sentence—sometimes that sentence would take the form of a single word—and letting Charlie speak several others before he spoke again.

It was charming—though it drove her crazy when it was directed at her. But since it wasn't now—and since he was engaging for her sake—she found it extra charming. Found *him* extra charming.

She'd been talking to another friend of Charlie's while said engaging was happening, but the woman had excused herself minutes ago, leaving Rosa to witness Charlie and Aaron's conversation. But it also gave her time to think. To consider what it meant that she'd told him the truth of why she'd left and he hadn't reacted the way she'd expected.

Except now that she'd told him, and had seen his reaction, she wasn't sure what her expectation had been. Had she thought he would agree to end things between them because she might be ill like her mother? Or had she expected him to stay, to support her, and *that* had been what she'd feared?

She didn't know. Both seemed equally fearsome to her now. Both seemed like valid arguments.

Because of what she'd been through with her mother, she still couldn't make a decision to save her life. Literally. She didn't want that for Aaron. Nor did she want him to go back to being afraid of life, of love because his life had taught him to be. Because the people in his life—because almost losing his mother—had forced him to protect himself.

Aaron's eyes met hers and he gave her a small, indulgent smile. Something swelled inside her. Guilt, she thought. Because, by leaving, she hadn't proven to Aaron that living and loving were worth it. Danger, too. Because something swelling inside her meant that she wanted to.

'Rosa, you've never watched *City Blue*?'

Her eyes flickered up to Charlie's, her mind taking a moment to play catch-up before she shook her head. 'No. Legal dramas are more Aaron's thing.'

'And what's your thing? *South Africa's Next Top Model*?' Charlie asked with a wry grin, but her gaze had already met Aaron's and they were both smiling when she answered.

'Yes, actually.'

Charlie looked between them. 'You're serious?'

'Rosa's a designer,' Aaron said. 'Shows like *South Africa's Next Top Model* are like drugs to her. Either she gets ideas for her new designs or she gets to picture herself designing the clothes the models wear.'

Charlie blinked, though Rosa couldn't tell whether it was because that was the most that Aaron had said during their conversation, or because he was surprised by the information her husband had supplied.

'I immediately regret my dismissive comment now,' Charlie said, rubbing a hand over the back of his neck.

'Don't worry,' Rosa said with a chuckle. 'It takes more than that to offend me.'

As she said it, the lights in the room flickered. Moments later, a woman walked into the hall and announced that the electrical grid was up and running one hundred per cent again.

'Storm's calming too,' Charlie said, looking up at the windows. There was barely a beat between his words and his radio crackling. He spoke in quick, short sentences and, by the time he was done, he offered them an apologetic smile.

'Duty calls. It was lovely meeting you both.' He shook their hands. 'When are you guys leaving?'

'Monday,' Aaron answered.

Charlie nodded. 'Well, shout if you need any more help. Though I wouldn't recommend shutting yourselves in rooms any more, okay?'

He gave them a quick smile before walking off, leaving a strange, not quite awkward but not easy silence behind him.

'We should probably get back too,' Aaron said finally.

'And I should find somewhere else to stay.' But she didn't move.

'You know you don't have to.'

Her gaze met his. 'You're…okay with having me there?'

He nodded. She bit her lip and wondered what she would be getting herself into if she agreed to go back to the house with him.

Danger.

Except not going back with him would be throwing away the progress they'd made that evening. She wasn't sure why that progress was suddenly so important—what did it matter, if she still intended to leave him when this was all over?—but it had her nodding and handing him the keys to the car.

They made the trip back to the house silently and when they pulled into the garage Rosa held her breath. She didn't know what to expect from him. Didn't know what *he* expected. And holding her breath seemed to help still the sudden drastic beating of her heart. And the sudden trembling anxiety in her stomach.

'We should go in.'

She forced herself to breathe. 'Yes.'

Silence pulsed between them for another few moments, and then he turned to her. 'How does a movie night sound?'

It was like old times. Which was probably a thought he should steer away from, especially since old times hadn't involved Rosa pressed against one side of the couch with him at the other.

Old times would have her curled up against him. Old times would have meant they wouldn't be resisting the electricity sparking between them. If it *had* been old times, Aaron would have pulled Rosa into his lap ages ago and done something constructive—something enjoyable—with the restless energy flowing through his veins.

But it *wasn't* old times. Though there *was* something between them now that hadn't been there before. He couldn't put his finger on what. Couldn't place how he felt about it. Or how the divorce discussion they'd had earlier had contributed to it.

How it had shifted something inside him. As though that something was desperately shunning even the *thought* of ending their marriage.

So he sat there, ignoring it all, pretending to watch the movie.

An explosion went off onscreen—the final one, thankfully—and the movie ended with a close-up of the hero and heroine kissing.

He rolled his eyes.

'You didn't like it?' Rosa asked with a slanted smile.

'I've seen better.'

'Yeah?' That smile was still in place. 'Like… *City Blue*?'

'Movies,' he clarified. '*City Blue* is a series.'

'And it doesn't compare?'

'It's much better than this.'

'Oh.' Her smile widened now, and his heart rate slowly increased.

'You're teasing me.'

'How can you tell?'

His lips curved. 'I've missed this.'

He cursed mentally when the easiness of their banter dissipated and her smile faded.

'Me too,' she replied softly after a few moments, and when their eyes met he swore he felt fire ignite between them.

Suddenly, he was reminded of that kiss they'd shared earlier. How it had been comfortable but had displaced something inside him. How it had soothed him just as it had spurred him on.

His fingers curled into his palms as he remembered how soft her skin had felt under them. As he remembered the way her curves felt. Slopes and indents and bumps unique to her that made his body ache and his heart race.

'Maybe…' she said hoarsely, before standing up slowly. She cleared her throat. 'Maybe I should make some tea.'

'The only kitchen that's stocked is the one on the top floor.' His voice was surprisingly steady.

'Okay. Just don't let the door shut behind us.'

She left him without checking that he was following and, a little helplessly, he did. He worried when a voice in his head questioned whether he'd follow her anywhere. Felt alarm when his heart told him he would.

Run, he told himself. It would be best to run, to get away from the temptation of her. But his feet kept following. And his eyes ran over the curves his hands had only just remembered touching.

She had swapped her jeans for pyjama pants he'd found in his cupboard, though she'd kept the top she'd worn earlier. The pants were baggy, ill-fitting, and yet he could picture the lower half of her body so clearly she might as well have been naked.

He shook his head and stayed at the door when they reached the top floor. He leaned against the wall. Watched her go through the motions of making tea.

'I didn't mean you have to stand there like a stalker,' she told him after putting on the kettle.

'I'm keeping the door from shutting.'

'Which I'd appreciate more if you didn't look like a creep doing it.'

He shifted his body. 'Better?'

Her lips curved. 'Was that your attempt at making yourself less creep-like?'

He smiled. 'It didn't work?'

She laughed. 'Not as well as I think you think it did.'

They smiled at each other, and then she drew her bottom lip between her teeth and turned away.

'Rosa?' he asked softly.

'It's nothing,' she replied. And then the click of the kettle went off and she sighed. 'I just… I keep thinking about what Doreen said about your mother. About how she did good things sometimes.'

He stiffened. 'What about it?'

'Well, don't you think that maybe this is one of those things?' She poured the water into two mugs, avoiding his eyes.

'I don't know what you mean.'

'You do.' Now she did meet his eyes, but she looked away just as quickly and replaced the kettle on its stand. 'But, since you're probably going to keep pretending you don't, I'll tell you.' She stirred the contents of the mugs before removing the tea-bags and adding milk. 'Bringing us together this weekend. Forcing us to talk.'

'She might have brought us here together, but she didn't force us to talk.'

'We both know it would have happened.'

'Not in the way it has.'

She walked to him with the two mugs, handed him his before switching off the lights. Everything went dark except for the stars in the sky, clear now that the rain had stopped.

'It really is beautiful up here,' she said after a moment. He looked around the room his mother had designed with an architect and grudgingly agreed.

'Better now that we're not trapped.'

'Yes,' she said, turning back to him. His eyes had adjusted to the darkness, allowing him to see her half-smile. His heart shuddered as their eyes held, and then she looked away. 'We should get back down before our tea gets cold.'

'You don't want to have it up here?'

'And have you stalk me while I drink it?' She smiled. 'No, thank you.'

His lips curved as he followed her down the stairs, careful not to spill the tea. She led them to the living area on the first floor. It was pretty here too, he thought, taking in the tasteful décor, the view of the beach through the windows.

His family had owned this house for decades, though his mother had made a lot of changes over the years. Some—like the top floor and the décor on the current floor—he'd agreed with. Others— like the incredibly excessive water feature she'd installed in the garden—she should have let go.

'I get that the talking is us,' she told him. Her expression was careful, and he wondered what she saw in his face when he hadn't realised she'd been watching him. 'But would we have talked if your mother hadn't tricked us into being here?'

He didn't reply immediately. 'I know that sometimes she means well.' It was almost painful to admit. 'But this—you and I—and Doreen… Those cases are few out of many.'

'Don't they count?'

He gripped the mug between his hands. 'My mother hopes for the best when she does things. She doesn't think them through.' He stilled. 'Those people she invited to live here could have been criminals. They could have taken everything in here. Or worse.'

He tried to relax his jaw, and then continued carefully. 'You have to think about the consequences of your actions. That's how life works.'

'Speaking as someone who can act without thinking about consequences,' she said slowly, 'I think you need to give her a break.'

'You might act impulsively sometimes, Rosa, but you don't expect other people to bear the brunt of those decisions.'

'Sometimes I do,' she said quietly. 'I have. With you.'

have done out eventually. And their relationship
would have crumbled down around them, just as
it had now.

'The tests,' she whispered as she moved.
'What—'

'I asked what I was so young, can I remember—'

if I wasn't worth the pain

still. I'd had she'd on me.

CHAPTER THIRTEEN

'WHAT DO YOU MEAN?' There was an urgency in the
question that had the answer spilling from her lips.

'Things would have been different for us if I'd
had that test done.'

'How?'

'I wouldn't have worried as much about the
lump. I wouldn't have felt as though I had to leave
to protect you from it. From me.' She rubbed her
arms. 'I wouldn't have doubted my decisions.
Every one of them, since my mother died.' She
laughed breathlessly. 'Since long before it, actually. But then it was for different reasons.' She
shook her head, hoping her words made sense to
him. She took a breath. 'We wouldn't be here if
I'd had that test done.'

'Wouldn't we?' was but

It was the only comment he made. She'd ripped
her heart out to tell him that—and that was all he
said.

Not that she could blame him. He was right.
Their relationship would have taken this turn eventually. There'd been too many things left unsaid between them. Too many cracks in their foundation.
Neither of them had noticed it before. But it would

have come out eventually. And their relationship would have crumbled down around them, just as it had now.

'I'm tired of hoping with my mother.'

'What?'

'It started when I was so young I can't remember anything other than the hope.' Something unreadable crossed his face. 'But, as I got older, I realised that I'd keep hoping, even when she'd prove to me that it wasn't worth the pain. Like when she got sick. I hoped she'd change.'

Understanding he was offering her something with this, she nodded. 'But she didn't.'

He shook his head. 'It wasn't that I was hoping for too much. I just wanted her to change her behaviour so I wouldn't have to keep fixing things for her. And—' he hesitated '—I wanted her to be there for me like I'd been there for her.' He paused. 'I put my life on hold when she found out she had cancer. It made me realise how much the fact that she was my mother meant to me, however complicated our relationship was. But even a life-changing event like cancer couldn't make *her* change.' Another pause. 'She used her *birthday* to manipulate us, knowing how important it would be to you.' He shook his head again. 'It's not as easy to forgive her as you've made it seem.'

She wondered what he would say if she told him that this was part of why she'd left. He'd never told her this before, but it had clarified things for her.

Because she'd sensed some of how he felt. Enough to understand that Aaron would have put his life on hold for her too, if she'd had cancer.

And if she'd had cancer she would have become the person she'd been running from her entire life. Anxious, bitter. Terrified of death. She would have become her mother.

The lump had catapulted her in that direction anyway. Had awoken the seed of fear she hadn't known had been buried inside her. But it had grown so quickly Rosa had known she couldn't stay. She couldn't let him see her become her mother. She couldn't let him go through that pain. Because now, hearing him say this… It made her fully appreciate how painful it would have been for him to be at her side.

'Aaron—'

'We should get to bed,' he said, not meeting her eyes. He set his mug down, his tea untouched.

'You don't want to—' She broke off when he sent her a beseeching look, and she nodded. He'd given her enough. He didn't want to talk about it any more. And, if she were honest with herself, neither did she.

'It's probably for the best to get to bed. To finally get a decent night's sleep.'

'You didn't sleep well last night?' he asked in a wry tone that sounded forced.

'It'll go better tonight, I'm sure.' After the briefest hesitation, she leaned over and brushed a kiss on his forehead. 'I'm sorry. For all of it.' She left before he could reply.

As she climbed into bed she heard Aaron's footsteps pass her door. When the sound stopped, she held her breath, anticipation fluttering through her. But then the footsteps continued, and she blew out the air she'd been holding in her lungs.

She wasn't sure why she'd reacted that way. Or what she would have done if Aaron had entered her room.

No, she thought, shutting her eyes. She knew *exactly* what she would have done.

And that was part of the problem.

When the sun woke Rosa the next morning, she wasn't surprised. Cape Town was famous for its unpredictable weather. And, since Mariner's Island was only thirty kilometres from Cape Town, the weather was pretty much the same there too.

Which was great, she mused, since the restlessness she'd felt the night before—when she'd thought Aaron might be coming into her room to seduce her—was still with her. But sunshine meant escape. And, right now, escape meant going for a run on the beach.

It wasn't ideal running gear, she mused as she looked at herself in the mirror. Most of what she was wearing had come from Liana's closet and, since her mother-in-law was smaller than her, the outfit wasn't quite appropriate for a run.

But the tank top would keep her boobs in place, and she'd replaced her ridiculous lace underwear with Liana's yoga tights. Again, not ideal, but it would have to do. Though she breathed a sigh of relief when she found a long, loose T-shirt of her own that would cover most of it.

When she'd tied her running shoes—Liana's— she stepped out of the room and made her way to the front door.

'Rosa?'

She spun around, her heart racing when she saw Aaron on the couch in the front room. His shirt was only half buttoned, revealing smooth muscular skin. It stopped just below his crotch, which she hadn't noticed before. Perhaps because, before, he'd been wearing *pants*.

She cleared her throat. 'You slept here last night?'

He lifted a hand to his hair and she fought to keep her eyes on his face. 'Yeah. None of the bedrooms were…comfortable.'

She nodded. 'I'm…er…going for a run.'

'A run?' He arched a brow. 'That bad, huh?'

She managed a smile. 'Just some restless energy.'

'Up for some company?'

She shook her head. 'It won't be for long.'

'Okay.'

Though his expression was unreadable, something in his tone gave her pause. And then it hit her. He hadn't been *uncomfortable*. He'd been watching out for her. He'd slept in the front room because he'd thought *that she might leave.*

Guilt knocked the breath from her and she forced herself out of the door before she did something about it.

He kept himself busy. Which was exactly what he'd done when she'd left the last time—so he wouldn't go crazy.

Now, though, it seemed ridiculous. He'd seen what she was wearing. And she'd left without any of her things. She wasn't *leaving*, leaving. Besides, where would she go? It was Sunday; the airport was still closed. She couldn't escape Mariner's Island even if she wanted to.

He clenched his jaw and continued preparing their breakfast. Ignored the voice that mocked him for being so desperate about not letting his wife leave him that he'd slept on the couch.

When he heard the front door open, the air began to move more easily in and out of his lungs. He made coffee and, by the time she came upstairs after a shower, had a cup ready for her.

'Did it work?' he asked as he handed her the cup. Her mouth curved. So, she wasn't going to pretend she didn't know what he was talking about.

'A little.'

'You were gone a while.'

'I was coming back.'

'I know.'

But something pulsed between them that confirmed she knew he hadn't been sure of it.

'How is it outside?'

She quirked a brow. 'Are we talking about the weather now?'

A faint smile claimed his lips as he nodded. 'Unless you have something else you want to talk about?'

'Oh, no,' she said dryly. 'The weather's fine. It's cool, with a south-easterly wind. Not quite swimming weather, folks.'

His smile widened. 'You sound exactly like her.'

'Cherry du Pont,' she said with a smile. 'The weather woman we listened to every morning for years.' She lifted a shoulder. 'I should hope I know what she sounds like.'

'Have you been listening to her by yourself?'

He wasn't sure what had made him ask it. And when she tilted her head, studied him, he was sure she didn't want to answer it. Surprise fluttered through him when she did.

'Some days. When I felt—' her eyes swept away from him '—when I felt lonely, or missed you.' She shifted away from the table, went to the glass door overlooking the beach. 'Most days, actually,' she continued. 'But then I'd force myself out of it, and start working. I managed to do an entire line that way.'

She gave him a cheeky smile over her shoulder and looked back at the beach before he could smile back. Good thing, as he wasn't going to smile back. No, he felt as if he could barely move, could barely *think* over her words echoing in his head.

When I...missed you... Most days...

He wanted to ask her why she hadn't come back then. Didn't she think they could be saved? Didn't she think that whatever she was going through they could go through *together*?

'It was because of you that I did it,' she said, breaking through his thoughts.

He cleared his throat. 'What was because of me?'

'The line.' She turned back now and walked to the stack of French toast he'd made earlier. She put two slices on a plate and squeezed honey over it.

'What does the line have to do with me?'

She looked at him and he saw understanding flood her eyes. She knew what her words had done to him. Perhaps that was why she kept talking.

'The line. For bigger women.' She went to the couch with her coffee and her toast.

He stacked his own plate with toast and bacon, and then went to sit opposite her. 'Why now?'

'I don't know.'

'Rosa.'

She looked at him. 'It's not an easy reason.'

His stomach clenched. 'Tell me.'

'I don't think—'

'Rosa,' he said again. He injected as much patience as he could into his tone, and unspoken words passed between them.

Tell me.

You won't like it.

Tell me anyway.

'I guess… Well, at first it was practical. And the reasons that had kept me from doing it were no longer much of an issue. Being a prominent lawyer's wife had done wonders for my own designs. And the people who wore them because of your mother.' She gave him a smile that was marked by sadness. 'Anyway, it seemed like the right time to do it.'

'At first,' he said quietly. 'You said at first.'

'And you would pick up on that, wouldn't you?' she asked in the same tone. But she nodded. 'It also…made me feel close to you.'

Surprise and emotion punched his heart. He nodded. 'Okay.'

'Okay,' she repeated, though it wasn't a question. And that was the last thing either of them said for a while.

They started eating in silence and by the time they'd finished their meal he realised it was his turn. He debated what would be the best way to tell her. Began speaking before he'd fully decided.

'The expansion,' he said, setting down his plate. 'It's a firm in Cape Town.'

'Cape Town?'

He nodded. 'Frank's been nagging me for a while. It seemed like the right time.'

They'd both used that phrase to explain what they'd been doing while they'd been away from one another. And now that Aaron had said it he realised that the 'right time' merely meant that they'd needed to occupy their time. With things that felt like work but reminded them of each other.

'In hindsight, maybe going for a run wasn't such a good idea,' Rosa said suddenly. He turned in time to see her set down her empty cup and plate and push back her hair. Her face was a bit pale and when she looked at him her eyes were dim.

'You're not feeling well?'

'I feel…off.' She shifted to the front of her seat. 'Though that could be because I went for a jog. It's…been a while.' She gave him a weak smile.

'You should rest.'

'Maybe,' she replied with a frown. And then she stood and when he saw that she wasn't entirely steady he moved beside her and told her to lean on him.

'This is probably an overreaction.' He grunted in response. 'I'm fine, really.'

He looked over at her as he led her to the bed. 'You're tired.'

'So are you.'

He grunted again.

'We're not letting each other sleep very well, are we?'

'You're going to sleep now.'

'That sounds like a threat.'

'It is.' But he smiled at her and said softly, 'Get some sleep.'

'Okay.'

He watched as she settled down. Felt an ache in his heart that he'd ignored for months but couldn't any more. He didn't know how long he sat at the edge of the bed, making sure she was okay. But when he shifted to leave he felt a hand on his forearm.

Her eyes were still closed when he looked back, but her grip on his arm was firm. And after a short moment of deliberation he let himself relax beside her.

A mistake, he knew instantly. There were boundaries, as she'd said, and he wanted now, more than ever, to keep those boundaries. He understood them. Because they didn't know where they stood with one another. *He* didn't know.

And, he considered as he held his breath as Rosa snuggled back against him, he didn't think she did either.

What he needed to do was get up and go downstairs. He needed to put distance between them. So that when, the next day, they left and went back to the separate lives they'd forged for themselves it wouldn't hurt as much.

And he thought it might not. Now that he knew the circumstances of why she'd left, he realised that it had less to do with him and more to do with her. Logically. Except it still *felt* as if it was to do with him. Just like he'd thought it was for every moment of those last four months.

Since he couldn't stop himself from feeling it, he figured there must be some truth in it, regardless of what she said. And, honestly, he couldn't blame her.

CHAPTER FOURTEEN

WHEN ROSA WOKE it wasn't entirely dark, but it wasn't light either. She took some time to realise that she'd slept most of the day away, and it was now dusk.

But it seemed the sleep had done its work. The fatigue she'd felt earlier had lifted somewhat and she didn't feel as listless. It wasn't a surprise that she'd felt that way. She had stepped into the rain like a fool—and she swore she'd feel the effects of that soon—and she hadn't slept well over the last two nights.

She should thank Aaron for forcing her to sleep, she thought, and then started when there was a movement next to her.

Her breath whooshed from her lungs. It was *Aaron*. Aaron was *sleeping beside her*. She searched her mind for any memory of how that had come to be, and nearly groaned when she remembered grabbing his arm as she'd fallen asleep.

It had been a reflex, and she hadn't meant much by it. No, she thought with a silent groan. That was a lie. Her sleepy self had just had the courage to do what she couldn't when she was awake.

Cling to him. Ask him not to leave her.

It was ridiculous, she told herself as she shifted so that she could see him better. She'd left him. And for good reasons too. Though, for the life of her, at that moment Rosa couldn't remember one of those reasons.

Her hand had lifted without her noticing it and now her fingers were tracing his forehead, down the side of his cheek. Her thumb brushed over his lips and her heart thudded at the memories of what those lips had done to her.

Moreover, it craved the healing those lips had done. How they'd kissed away her tears when her mother had died. How they'd comforted her as he'd kissed her temple at her mother's funeral.

She'd got through so much because he'd been there for her. Those lips, kissing, comforting, yes, but because of *him*. Because of his presence. Because of his steadfastness.

She blinked at the tears that burned in her eyes and her hand lowered. Over the curve of his Adam's apple, into the cleft at the base of his neck. Her fingers fluttered over the collarbone on each side, before resting between them. He wore another shirt, though this one was flannel, the kind she knew he wore on casual occasions.

The top buttons were open and she saw her fingers shake more as they scooped down to the edge of the skin that those buttons revealed. It was just enough for her to see the slope between his pecs, and she remembered all the times she'd rested her head there, listening to his heart, being calmed by it.

Without thinking about it, she undid another button and was about to slide her hand in, so that she could feel his heart again—so that she could have that calmness again—when his fingers closed over hers.

She sucked in her breath, felt her skin flush with the embarrassment of being caught caressing the man she'd left while he was sleeping.

'What are you doing?' His voice was husky, sexy, sending a shiver down her spine.

'Nothing,' she replied, breathier than she wanted.

'It didn't feel like nothing.' His eyes opened and she nearly gasped at the need she saw there. At that intense look in his eyes that had always meant one thing.

Resist.

But she could feel herself falling.

'It…wasn't nothing,' she said helplessly. She tugged at the hand he held in his grip, but he wouldn't let go.

'What was it?'

'Memories,' she whispered, giving up now. She flattened her hand under his, let her fingers spread across his chest.

'Of…us?'

'Of you. And how often you've made me feel… better than I should.'

'When?'

'Always.'

'That can't be true.'

'It is.' She took a breath and shifted up so that their eyes were in line with one another's. 'You know now that I didn't leave because of you.'

His eyes darkened and his other arm went around her waist, pressing her closer to him. It was seduction, though she didn't understand how it could be.

'No.'

'Aaron—'

'Rosa.' His expression was serious and she stopped herself from interrupting him, knowing that he needed to speak. 'You left because there was something about me that you didn't want.'

'I left because I didn't want you to see how broken I was,' she corrected him softly, and used her free hand to press against his cheek. 'I didn't want you to be me and I didn't want me to be—'

'Your mother.'

'Yes.'

'You didn't have to leave,' he said after a moment.

'I know. And if I'd told you whatever I was feeling you would have told me that too. But I know you. And I know that you're…committed to making things better for other people.'

'I'm committed to you,' he replied simply. 'You're my wife.'

'And that's why I had to leave. I didn't want you

to have to...to have to be responsible for me too. To take care of me when you shouldn't have to.'

'That's what you thought?' He pushed himself up against the pillows. 'You thought that this—us— would somehow end up being like the relationship between me and my mother?'

'I didn't at the time,' she admitted softly. 'Up until last night, I don't think I did. I thought I was doing it because I was saving you from something. Protecting you from being me in the relationship I had with my mother. But I see now that part of it was just trying to keep you from...from being *you*.'

His face tightened and a pain she didn't understand shone in his eyes. 'I'm sorry.'

'Why are you apologising?' she demanded, unsteady from the emotion.

'I've made you cry.' His hand lifted to brush the tears from her cheeks.

She blew out a breath. 'That wasn't you.'

'Hard to convince me of that when you're crying in my arms while talking to me.' He smiled, but it wasn't the easy smile he usually gave her. And it...bothered her.

'Aaron, it's never you.' She moved again, and this time she propped her head on his chest, on her hands, and looked him in the eye. 'You're the best thing that's ever happened to me.'

He nodded, though she didn't think he believed her. She was about to open her mouth to try and make him understand again when he looked beyond her and a more genuine smile claimed his lips.

'We might just have weathered a bad storm on Mariner's Island, but that won't keep the locals from celebrating.'

She followed his gaze and sat up with a gasp when she saw the fireworks go off on the beach. Though it was some distance away, they could see it clearly and the silence as they watched made the tension following their conversation settle.

She leaned back against him and sighed with pleasure at the simplicity of the moment. Somewhere in her mind she thought that perhaps she hadn't only been tracing the shape of his face, letting the memories wash over her when he'd been sleeping. No, now she thought that she'd been memorising it. Just like she was memorising that very moment so she could go back to it some day.

And with that thought something loosened inside her and, though her mind told her it was a terrible decision, she ignored it. Much like she ignored every warning it would give her when she was about to do something rash. When she was about to do something possibly stupid.

'You never needed an excuse, you know,' she said, turning to him and moving until she was sitting on her knees facing him.

'For what?' he asked carefully.

'To kiss me.'

His eyes went hot. Seduction, she thought again. 'You mean I don't have to dance with you to kiss you?'

'Yes.'

'Okay.' But he didn't move.

She cleared her throat. 'That was an invitation.'

'I know.'

'So…?'

He shook his head. 'You don't need an excuse either. If you want me to kiss you, you're going to have to do it yourself.'

She understood why he wanted that from her. He wanted her to make the decision. He wanted her to cross the line. Which was fair, she considered. He'd kissed her the first time, when they'd been dancing. And she'd been the one who had put the line there in the first place.

With an exaggerated sigh, she leaned forward and slid a hand behind his head. 'Just like our first kiss,' she whispered as she brought her lips closer to his. 'Seems like I have to do everything myself.'

And then they were kissing—falling—and it didn't matter who'd started it, only that they had.

He hated himself for what he was about to do. Hated it because he'd slept on a couch the night before to prevent *her* from doing it. But he didn't have a choice. And though the voice in his head told him that that was a lie—that it was an excuse and he *did* have a choice—he was going to do it anyway.

With one last look at Rosa sleeping naked beside him—accepting the longing, the guilt—Aaron got up and made a few calls. Then he packed everything he'd brought with him and forced himself to leave the house without saying goodbye to her.

She'd understand, he told himself as he got into his car and drove away from the house—from his wife. She'd understand that he couldn't deal with what had just happened between them. What he saw now had been inevitable from the moment he'd seen her—in that gold dress, in her sexy shapewear, in his shirt, her jeans, that running gear.

From their *kiss*.

But she'd understand that he couldn't deal with the intimacy, the passion, the *love* that had been clear in what they'd just done. That he didn't want any of it to be spoilt by a discussion of what would happen next.

So he'd left.

It was Monday morning—early, yes, but the airport would be open—so he *could* leave. He'd called his plane and, though it would take some time for it to get there, he'd rather wait at the airport than at the house. With the prospect of Rosa waking up. Realising what was happening. The inevitable confrontation. The inevitable conversation…

He was trying to avoid all that. For both of them. He would be saving them both from the pain, the heartache.

So why did he still hate himself for doing it?

CHAPTER FIFTEEN

IT HAD BEEN a month since Aaron had left her alone in that bed. A month since they'd made love. A month since she'd woken up to find herself naked and alone.

The last thing Rosa wanted was to be in Aaron's office now, *especially* thinking of that weekend. It made the fact that *he'd* left *her* this time worse than when she'd left him.

At least that was what she told herself.

But she *had* to think of it in that way. In *any* way that would make her feel better about the turn her life had taken in the last month. If she'd had a choice, she'd still be in Cape Town. Safe, away from Aaron. She'd still be working on her line. On her life.

Instead, she was in Johannesburg, in her husband's office—*the husband who'd left her alone and naked after they'd made love*—waiting for him so that she could tell him her news and return to that life she'd created for herself in Cape Town.

Her stomach tumbled when she thought that that might not happen after she told Aaron her news.

The door opened, distracting her as Aaron entered the room. Just as handsome as ever, she thought. More so when he was surprised. She almost smiled at his widened eyes. At the way he tensed.

Good.

And then her stomach heaved in a way that had nothing to do with nerves, and she gritted her teeth. She would do this without throwing up. She couldn't give him that power too.

'Rosa,' he said in a calm tone, but she heard the subtle quaking. 'What are you doing here?'

Fairly certain the contents of her stomach were back where they belonged, she replied, 'I've come to see you, darling husband.' She stood up—dramatic flair had always made her feel more confident. 'At least that was what I told your secretary. Turns out he still believes we're a married couple.'

'Of course he still believes it,' he said in a low voice, closing the door behind him. He set his briefcase on the chair next to the door and walked directly to his bar. 'That's what we are.'

'Could have fooled me,' she said through her teeth. 'I didn't realise married couples left each other naked after a passionate night of reconciliation without so much as a word.'

His skin darkened slightly. 'Don't.'

'Why not?'

'You're not as innocent as you're making it seem.'

He took a healthy sip of the alcohol. Jealousy stirred inside her. She would have liked to have something to dull her nerves before she told him. Hell, she would have liked to dull everything inside her. Except, in her current state, she couldn't.

Which brought her back to the real reason she was there.

'Fortunately, I'm not here to discuss the tit-for-tat turn our marriage has taken,' she said swiftly. She walked around the desk, stood closer to the door. Closer to escape when she needed it.

'Then why are you here?'

'Because it seems our—' she swallowed and told herself it would be best just to get it out '—because our night together has led to a…consequence.'

'What con—?' He cut himself off, his eyes lowering to her stomach, and she resisted an urge to put her hand on her abdomen. She wasn't sure where that urge had come from. She'd been strangely detached from the news that there was a life growing inside her since she'd found out. Detached. Alone. The way that life had come to be—how *that* had ended—was the only explanation she could think of for why she felt that way. Or the only explanation she *allowed* herself to think of.

'Are you…' he started, and then his voice faded before he cleared his throat. 'Are you telling me you're pregnant, Rosa?'

'Yes.'

She straightened her shoulders. Drew up her spine. This was the reason she'd worn another one of her designs. Confidence. Courage. This time it came in the form of high-waisted pants and a blue shirt.

'How…how… Are you sure?'

She'd rarely seen her husband so frazzled. 'I've taken multiple pregnancy tests.' And had hated herself for it. It seemed like something her mother would have done. 'And had it confirmed by my GP. It's still early, as you can imagine. But it's there.'

'But…how did this happen?'

'I wasn't taking the Pill any more. It didn't seem necessary.'

He made a disbelieving noise. It felt as if he'd slapped her. '*What?*'

'I didn't say anything,' he snapped, and began to pace the length of the room.

'No, you didn't,' she said. 'But that sound you made implied something. Almost as if getting pregnant was some kind of plan. As if the unwilling and unknowing part I played in your mother's misguided fairy tale plan was meant to end up like *this.*'

Her stomach turned again and she held up a finger when he opened his mouth, pressing her other hand to her own mouth. The wave of nausea had barely passed before another took its place and she strode to the door of his bathroom——thank heaven it was adjoined to Aaron's office——barely making it to the toilet in time to empty her stomach.

Which was strange, she thought as she heaved, since the only thing she'd managed to choke down that morning was a dry piece of toast and black rooibos tea. But there it went, followed by a few extra lurches of her stomach.

She flushed the toilet and sank down to the floor. It was refreshingly cool, though a moment later she felt an even colder cloth pressed to her forehead. She knew it was him before she opened her eyes. Saw the concern—and something else she couldn't place—on his face.

'I'm fine,' she said and tried to stand, incredibly aware of the fact that she hadn't rinsed her mouth. Steady hands helped her up and, exhausted, she couldn't summon the energy to be annoyed at his assistance.

She'd expected it, hadn't she? It was part of why she'd left him in the first place. Because she hadn't wanted this to be her life—to be his—if she were sick like her mother.

Ignoring the irony that had brought them to this point anyway, she asked him to get her handbag. And when he left gave herself a moment to take a quick breath before she washed her face and patted it down with the dry end of the towel he'd given her.

She was pale, she thought as she looked at herself in the mirror. The skin under her eyes looked bruised, and the light brown of her hair somehow looked darker because of it.

But she told herself not to be too concerned about it. She'd already been there, worrying about all the possibilities that had made her look and feel that way. It had pushed her into making an appointment with a psychologist, but then she'd missed her period and postponed *that* appointment in lieu for one with her GP.

Aaron returned with her handbag, and thankfully gave her space when she rummaged around in it to find the travel toothbrush and toothpaste she'd started carrying when throwing up had become the norm.

She made quick work of it, and then took another breath before walking out to face Aaron again.

'Better?' he asked in a clipped tone. She frowned. How had she possibly annoyed him by throwing up?

'For now,' she answered mildly. 'You?'

His expression darkened, and there was a long pause before he said, 'I'm sorry. I shouldn't have reacted that way.'

'You didn't really react. Besides when you implied that I somehow tricked you into making me pregnant.' At his look, she shrugged. 'You know that's how you made it seem. And, if I recall, you were as much into the activity that got us here as I was.'

Though she hadn't thought it possible, he looked even more peeved than he'd been before. Not that it surprised her. She was purposely being contrary, but it was the only way she could cope with what was happening. And again, she'd give herself permission to do just about anything if it helped her cope.

'Does this mean you're not accepting my apology?' he asked quietly, and she lifted her shoulders. 'Rosa,' he said more insistently now, and she blew out a breath.

'Yes. Fine. I accept your apology.'

He folded his arms and leaned against his desk, looking at her evenly. Back to being in control, she thought, resenting it.

'What did you hope to achieve by coming here today?' he asked.

She frowned. 'I didn't hope to achieve anything. I just came to let you know.'

'You came all the way to Johannesburg to let me know that you're pregnant?'

'Yes. Or would you have liked that information over the phone?'

He didn't react to her sarcasm. 'Thank you for coming to tell me in person.' He paused. 'But I suppose what I'm actually asking is whether this was a planned trip, or whether it was spur-of-the-moment?'

It *had* been spur-of-the-moment, something she'd convinced herself to do before she lost the nerve. So she'd booked the ticket, put on the sample suit she'd made for her line, and now she was here.

But she wouldn't tell him that.

'I came here to tell you that you're going to be a father,' she said, and saw that he wasn't as unaffected as he was pretending to be. 'Other than that... Well, no, I suppose I didn't know what else *to* achieve.'

'But you didn't think you were going to tell me and then just leave?'

Her heart started thudding, reminding her of when he'd said something similar when she'd first arrived at the house on Mariner's Island. 'I know we have to talk about things.'

'Yes,' he agreed. 'But more than that, Rosa. We're going to have to fix this marriage.'

She inhaled sharply, and then let the air out between her teeth before she replied.

'That's a high expectation from someone who didn't have any intention of doing that a month ago.'

'Did you?' he asked softly, the haughtiness of her statement not putting him off. In fact, it did the exact opposite. It told him that she was scared. And he'd contributed to that fear by leaving.

'Did I what?'

'Did you have any intention of fixing things between us after we slept together?'

She opened her mouth and then cleared her throat. It was enough of an answer. Enough that he didn't need her to say anything else.

'So I was right to make it easier on the both of us by leaving.'

'Oh, is that why you did it?' Her eyebrows rose.

'I thought you left because you wanted to make me know how it felt to be the one left behind.'

'I'm not that vindictive.'

'I didn't think so either. But I had to wonder. Karma, and all that.' She was throwing his words from the first night on the island back at him. Then she abruptly changed the topic. 'Your mother called me.'

'You...you didn't tell her?'

'No. I didn't answer, actually. And then she sent an email saying she hadn't heard from you since you got back. Asked me whether that was some form of payback. Karma?' she asked lightly.

Annoyance bristled through him. 'You know better than to listen to my mother.'

'She's right about some things, Aaron,' she said. 'She was right to bring us to that island.'

'Look where that got us.'

Her hand shifted, moving towards her stomach before she jerked it back. Something about the movement irked him. 'Yes, we're in a...situation now, but this situation is proof that we couldn't just walk away from things and hope to never face them again.'

'I didn't walk away f—'

'First?' she interrupted him. 'Yes, I know I did that. And I know that I was wrong to do that, especially without any explanation.' She bit her lip, and then blew out another breath. 'I saw that on Mariner's Island when we were talking. And I realised that I should have told you about what I was going through so that, at the very least, we were on the same page.'

Why was she being so calm now? He almost preferred the haughtiness.

'So you would have tried to fix things between us?'

'No,' she said after a moment. 'But I would have tried to make you understand why I couldn't. So that when we walked away from one another I'd be able to move forward with a clear conscience. We both would.'

'Is that what you want to do now?' he forced himself to ask. Was proud of how he'd managed to ask it without revealing the emotion that was choking him.

'Partly, yes. We have even more reason to be on the same page now. Without the past clouding things.'

'What does that mean, Rosa?' He pushed off from the table. Took a step closer to her. 'What do *you* really mean?'

'We can't fix this,' she said stiffly. 'So maybe your idea of ending things—of filing for divorce—was for the best.'

how she wanted a divorce.

CHAPTER SIXTEEN

HE WASN'T EMOTIONALLY prepared to hear that Rosa
wanted a divorce. Hell, he wasn't emotionally prepared for *anything* that had happened in his office
since he'd walked in and found her there.

He'd been on somewhat of a high when he'd got
there too. The case he was working on was a particularly dirty one. The husband had more than
enough money and power to force his wife into di-
vorcing him quietly. And he would have succeeded
too, if Aaron had agreed to be *his* lawyer.

But the moment Aaron had met the man he'd
known no measure of money or power could make
Aaron represent him. Instead, he'd reached out to
the man's wife and had offered to take on her case
pro bono.

It had been a rocky ride—would be for some
time—but that day the judge had ruled on custody. And since the husband was the ass Aaron
thought he was, he'd gone for full custody based
solely on the fact that his wife wanted the kids. But
that day the wife had won. *They'd* won. And it had
felt *damn* good.

Until he'd seen the wife he'd walked out on a

month ago, found out she was pregnant and that now she wanted a divorce.

It was his own fault. He'd mentioned it before. And that had set the events in motion that had culminated in their night of passion.

But she *was* right. Things were hanging mid-air between them, and they couldn't live like that for ever. Particularly not if they were going to raise a child together.

A child.

He pushed the thought aside and told himself it wasn't the time to think about that. Or to remember how disappointed he'd been when she'd told him about the milk duct in her breast—the lump—and that that hadn't meant she was pregnant.

One problem at a time.

Since he'd had an appointment shortly after Rosa had dropped her bombshell, he'd had to deal with work first. But they'd arranged to have dinner together that night. So they could talk about *getting on the same page.*

She was already there when he arrived, and he fought the feeling of nostalgia at seeing her there. The restaurant had been his suggestion—it was the first one that had come to mind. Unfortunately, it was also one they'd been to often when they were together. And often she'd be waiting for him to get there.

Except then she'd had a smile on her face. Her expression would be open, warm, as soon as she saw him. That was not the case now. His heart took a tumble when he saw her wary expression. The tightness, the nerves. He'd done that, he thought again, and then forced it aside and took his seat.

'You came,' she said after a moment.

'You thought I wouldn't?'

'I...wasn't sure. After what happened today.'

'We don't have many choices any more, Rosa. You and I are in this together, whether you like it or not.'

She winced, but nodded. She was still pale, and when the waiter took their drinks order she asked for black tea and water. Not her usual.

'How are you feeling?'

Her eyes lifted. 'Fine.' They were tired. And he knew that she was lying.

'Rosa.'

'What?'

'If we're going to have this conversation, then we should be honest.'

Colour flooded her cheeks but she nodded. 'It hasn't been the best experience.'

'Obviously you're suffering from morning sickness.'

'Obviously,' she repeated dryly. 'And I'm tired. Even when I wake up. Par for the course.' She lifted her shoulders, but the gesture looked heavy and a sympathy he didn't understand pooled in his belly. A fear too.

He frowned. 'I'm sorry.'

She opened her mouth and then caught him off-guard with the smile that formed there. 'I was going to say it's not your fault, but then I realised it's at least fifty per cent your fault.'

His lips curved. 'I suppose.'

Her gaze suddenly sharpened, and then she released a breath. 'It is yours.'

It took him a moment to figure out how to reply. 'I didn't think it wasn't.'

She nodded. 'I know some... Well, thank you for not doubting that.'

'Things might not be in the best state between us,' he said stiffly, 'but I don't suddenly think that you've changed.'

'And changing would be sleeping with someone else?'

The air was charged, but he couldn't tell if it was because of her words or because of the way things were between them.

'Changing would be lying to me.'

And she'd never done that, he thought, seeing the confirmation of it on her face. At least there was that. They'd had honesty between them for the longest time. And if somehow that had changed it was just as much his fault as it was hers.

It might very well have been his fault alone.

'I'm sorry,' he said after the waiter brought their drinks. He waved the man away when he mentioned food, seeing Rosa recoil at the suggestion. 'I shouldn't have left you the way that I did.'

'Why did you?'

'I already told you.'

'You told me that you left because I was going to leave.' She was watching him closely. He shifted. 'I don't believe that, Aaron.'

'You should. It's the truth.'

'Not the whole truth.' She paused. 'If you've changed your mind about being honest...'

He clenched his teeth and then reached for his drink, which thankfully had alcohol in it. He nearly hissed as the liquid burnt down his throat and then he pushed it aside, no longer interested in the courage it offered.

Fake courage, he thought, since he still had to steel himself to answer her question.

'It seemed easier.' He didn't look at her. 'And what we shared...was special. To me, at least.' He paused. 'I knew that whatever we'd say to each other about it would spoil that, and I didn't want that memory to be destroyed. So I left.'

She took a long time to answer him. Because of that, he forced himself to look at her face. Her expression was unreadable, though her hands trembled slightly as she put some sugar into the tea in front of her, stirring the liquid much longer than it required.

'You're right,' she said eventually. 'It would have.' The stirring stopped. 'But then, I don't think you leaving the next day did much different.'

She lifted her eyes and their gazes met. Clashed.

But in them Aaron saw the acknowledgement that what they'd shared *had* been special. He didn't know if the effect that had on his heart was good or bad, all things considered.

'I'm sorry.'

She lifted her hand, as if to brush his apology away, and then dropped it again with a nod. 'Okay. It's in the past. Let's move on.'

There was an expectant pause after those words, as if she were waiting for him to say something that would do just that. Except he couldn't. Not immediately. His thoughts were too closely linked to the past. His feelings too.

He fought through.

The child.

'What are we going to do about the baby?'

She'd lifted her cup to her lips, but lowered it slowly after his question. Still, her hand shook. He resisted the urge to lean over and grip it.

'We're going to have it.' He nodded. He hadn't been concerned about that. He knew where they both stood on that issue. 'But, other than that, I... I don't know.'

Her grip tightened on the cup and he watched as she forcibly relaxed it.

'So let's take it one step at a time,' he said slowly. The temptation to make the decisions for her—to take the pain of it away from her—was strong. 'Your pregnancy.'

'Yes.' She blew out a breath.

'Where do you want to live during that time?'

'I…haven't thought about it. I have a flat in Cape Town. I suppose I'll live there.'

Panic reared its head, but he reined it in. 'Okay. Do you have friends out there?'

She gave him a strange look. 'Yeah, a few.'

'So they'd be able to help you through…this.'

'I suppose. I mean—' She broke off. 'It's not their responsibility.' He waited as she processed it, and then she sighed. 'Not this again.'

'What?'

'You know what, Aaron.' She pushed away her cup. 'You're trying to make me think that this—that I am your responsibility. I thought we were over that. I'm not your responsibility. I make my own choices.'

'I didn't say that you don't,' he replied with a calmness he didn't feel. Her words spoke to that inexplicable fear he'd had since seeing her on the ground after she'd thrown up at his office. After she'd told him how poorly she was feeling now. 'But didn't you tell me that I'm at least fifty per cent responsible for this?'

She narrowed her eyes. 'I hate that you're a lawyer.'

He smiled thinly.

'So, what?' she asked, wishing with all her might that she could wipe that smile off his face. 'You're saying that you want me to move back here? To go through my pregnancy here?'

'It's an option.'

'No. No, it's not.' She shook her head, and then rested it in her hands when the movement caused her head to spin. She shut her eyes, and then opened them again in time to see a drop of water fall onto the tablecloth.

She lifted one hand to her face and realised that the water was coming from her eyes. Was she crying? Damn it, she thought, and pushed her chair back, determined to make it to the bathroom before it became obvious.

But her head spun again when she stood, and pure panic went through her when she thought she'd fall down in the middle of the restaurant. But steady hands caught her and soon she was leaning against a rock-solid body.

'I'm fine,' she said but it sounded faint, even to her.

He didn't say anything, only lowered her back into her chair. Then he gestured for the waiter.

'What are you doing?' she asked through the spinning. 'We're not done yet.'

'No,' he agreed, his face etched with concern. 'But we'll continue some other time. You need rest.'

'There is no other time,' she said and closed her eyes. When he didn't reply, she opened them again. He was watching her with an expression that told her he wouldn't indulge her, and then he was speaking to the waiter and settling the bill.

Soon he was helping her up and out of the restaurant.

She wanted to pull away and tell him that she could walk by herself. But she wasn't sure that was the truth. The last thing she wanted was to fall down and make herself look even more of the fool. It was bad enough that she was basically being carried out of the restaurant.

'You can call me a taxi,' she said when they got outside. The air was crisp, and it helped to clear her head.

'You can ride with me.'

She debated wasting her energy on arguing with him, and then nodded. 'Fine. I'm at the Elegance Hotel.'

'You'll stay with me.'

'Aaron—'

'It's just one night,' he said, cutting off her protest. 'For one night you can stop fighting and just come home.'

Home. It sounded amazing, even though she wasn't entirely sure where home was any more. And perhaps it was because that made her think of her mother and sadness rolled over her in waves. Or perhaps it was because he'd been referring to *their* home and longing and nostalgia went through her.

Or perhaps it was just because his face was

twisted in an expression she'd never seen on him before. And the concern—the only emotion she could identify in that expression—was as strong as on the day he'd been beside her when she'd buried her mother.

Whatever it was—all of it, most likely—it had her agreeing.

'My flight leaves tomorrow evening.'

His expression tightened, but he nodded. 'Fine.'

'Fine,' she repeated as she got into his car. And then she closed her eyes and wished she were anywhere in the world but there.

CHAPTER SEVENTEEN

AARON COULDN'T HELP the ripple of anger that went through him as he remembered how helpless Rosa had looked at that restaurant. It took him some time to realise the cause, and even then he could only put his finger on one small thing: the fact that he'd let things go too far.

He shouldn't have slept with her. He knew that and yet, every time he thought back to the day it had happened, he didn't see how he could have avoided it.

They'd somehow woven a spell around themselves that weekend. Though he didn't know how that spell had gone from hurt and accusation to a deeper understanding of their issues. Their fears.

What had been missing in their marriage to make them end up like that? It had gone so wrong, and he'd thought things had been *good* between them. But clearly there'd been layers they'd barely explored.

Those questions had kept him up at night, and each time the buck had stopped with him. And he'd been forced to realise that he'd been doing something wrong. That maybe his approach of keeping his thoughts, his feelings to himself until Rosa extracted them from him had been wrong.

He'd got it wrong. Again.

He still felt the stirring of anger when he pulled into his driveway, though now it was tainted with guilt that tightened in his stomach. He took a breath and then got out of the car, moving to the other side so that he could carry Rosa into the house.

But she was already opening her door when he got there. The look in her eyes had anger and guilt spinning in his body again, making tracks he didn't think would ever go away.

Her gaze met his, and there was a recognition there that was replaced so quickly with caution that it did nothing for the way the emotions churned inside him.

'I can walk.'

He didn't reply. Instead, he stepped aside and waited for her to get out, standing close enough that if she needed him he'd be there. It sounded like a metaphor of some kind, but he couldn't find the energy to figure it out.

She staggered slightly when she stood, and she braced herself with a hand against his chest. And then she looked at her hand, removed it and straightened.

'Thank you,' she mumbled. He made a non-committal noise in response. He waited for her to walk in front of him, and then followed. He didn't bother guiding her. He'd driven to their house; she knew her way around.

He watched as she left her handbag on the kitchen counter, kicked off her shoes and took off her jacket, hanging it on the coat rack. It was so familiar his heart stuttered, nearly stopped. He needed to get a grip.

But then, it *was* his fault. He'd been the one to bring her here. And then she went straight to the couch, sat there gingerly, and he knew he'd made the right decision.

'What can I get you?'

'Nothing.' Then she shook her head. 'Actually, I didn't get to finish my tea, and that's about all I can keep down these days.'

He nodded and went to the kitchen to make her tea. He made himself a cup of coffee, thinking that he'd had enough to drink, though a part of him disagreed.

He handed her the tea and then sat down on the adjacent couch. There was a moment of silence, when he thought they were both thinking about how weird it was. The last time they'd been there together, they'd been happy. Or not, he thought, reminding himself that the last time they'd been there together, she'd left.

His hands tightened on the coffee mug.

'I really would have been okay,' she said into the silence.

He acknowledged her words with a nod. She bit the side of her lip, held the mug between her hands.

'Thank you.'

'You're welcome.'

More silence. They should go to bed, he thought. But now, with her there, going to bed didn't feel right. Not to the bed they'd shared, and not to any of the other rooms in the house. Because she was there. She should be with him. In his bed. In *their* bed.

He hadn't spent much time there in the four months she'd been gone. He'd worked late, stayed at the office as long as he could stay awake. And when he did come home he'd sleep on the couch she was now sitting on, unable to go to their bedroom alone.

When he'd returned from Mariner's Island, he'd tried. Told himself that he had to, since *he* was the one who'd made the decision to leave now. But when he hadn't been able to sleep for the fifth night in a row, he'd realised that he hadn't made that decision at all. That it hadn't been a decision. More, it had been a defensive move. He'd leave before she left him. Again.

The thought made him nauseous.

'I'll think about staying here.' She broke the silence again. 'Which was probably your plan all along.'

'My plan would have involved more than you just staying here,' he told her. 'But I appreciate it.'

'You knew I'd agree. You've been much too quiet...'

The corner of his mouth lifted. 'It's not that easy.'

'No.' She sighed. 'But you're right. I don't have people there. Not like I do here.'

'Then why did you go there?'

If she was surprised by the question, she didn't show it. 'I didn't really have much of a plan when I left here.'

'Spur of the moment.'

Now her lips her curved. 'Partly. But mostly it was me trying to run from what scared me most. Then,' she added almost as an afterthought, and he watched again as her hand lifted, almost moving to her stomach, and then dropping back to the mug again.

'And now?' he asked softly, compelled by her gesture.

'Now I have much more to fear.' The vulnerability in her eyes when she met his gaze knocked the breath from his lungs.

'You don't have to be scared of it. Of this.'

'Of course I do. There's so much we don't know. And this wasn't planned—'

'Isn't that when you work best?'

'Not with this. Not ever, really.' She frowned. 'I don't do the unplanned because I don't want a plan. I like plans. But for most of my life, plans haven't worked out. Or they involved things I wanted to do but that my mother's illness…' She trailed off. 'I had to be flexible. Or rebellious.'

'And…marrying me?' He forced himself to say it. 'Were you being rebellious?'

She didn't say anything for long enough that he thought their conversation was over. He was about to stand up, excuse himself when she started speaking.

'I've done a lot that I've called spontaneous. I probably would have continued calling it that if it hadn't been for our conversations. On the island. Now.' She ran a finger over the rim of her cup. 'The right word would probably be rebellious. Because that's what I was.' She lifted her eyes to his. 'Small moments of rebellion against the fact that I couldn't control so much of what was happening in my life.'

He breathed in slowly, deliberately letting the air in and out of his lungs. If he didn't, he'd probably pass out waiting for her to speak.

'Because of it, whatever I chose to do felt wrong. Whether I did it for myself or for my mother.' Her gaze fell again. 'If I did it for myself, guilt and uncertainty followed me. If I did it for my mother, it…wouldn't change anything. She'd still be sick.' She paused. 'Even after she died, I was rebelling. I didn't get the test because of it. And now I have to live with the guilt and uncertainty of that decision.'

She took a breath. 'I did things that weren't

planned. Rebelled. But marrying you—loving you—was never part of that.'

The air he inhaled grew thicker, though by all rights it should have been easier to breathe. She'd told him their relationship hadn't been a mistake. Yes, things had fallen apart towards the end, but at the beginning things had been good. So why didn't that make him feel any better?

Maybe it was because all he could think about was how she'd told him she'd left because of *him*. Because of who he was.

He'd thought about that often over the past five months. Had figured it was the reason his mother hadn't responded to his efforts to make a better relationship with her too. It was probably why his father—

No. That made no sense. He didn't know his father. His father didn't know him.

His father not being around had nothing to do with him.

Except maybe it did.

'Aaron?'

It was messing with him. This whole thing was messing with him.

'It's been a rough day,' he said gruffly. 'We should get some rest.'

She opened her mouth, but then nodded. 'I'll take one of the spare bedrooms.'

'No. Take the main bedroom.'

'That's not—'

'Rosa,' he said firmly. 'Take the main bedroom.'

She let out a breath. 'Okay. I'll see you in the morning.'

She disappeared around the corner to the passage that led to the bedroom, and Aaron waited until he heard the click of the door before moving. But, instead of walking to the room he'd planned on spending the night in, he went to the sliding door, opening it to let the fresh winter air in.

He stepped outside onto the deck that gave him a perfect view of the dam the houses in their security estate had been built around. He'd known he wanted to live there the moment he'd seen it. And when one of his clients who knew the owner of the security estate had given him the details, Aaron had jumped at the opportunity to buy a property.

Months later, it had been his and Rosa's.

His and Rosa's. He'd taken that fact for granted. He'd believed that they were going to be a unit, a him-and-her-for-ever. But he'd been sorely mistaken. He realised now how often that happened. How he'd ignored it to protect himself.

He'd been mistaken when he'd thought his mother would change after recovering from cancer. That she'd be more responsible. That she'd begin to value her only son.

He'd been mistaken when he'd thought his wife would be with him for ever. When he'd believed that she hadn't left because of him—as she'd led him to believe in the early part of their visit on the island.

He'd been mistaken when he'd slept with her. When he'd been so overcome by the love he still had for her that he'd let his feelings cloud his judgement.

And now he was here—so raw that he felt as if he were made entirely of abused nerve-endings. What was wrong with him that the people in his life didn't want him? What more could he do to make them love him as much as he loved them?

He hung his head as the pain crawled through him. As it ripped its nails down him as on a chalkboard.

Because the answer was simple. He *couldn't* do anything more. Because nothing he did would change who he was. And who he was wasn't enough.

CHAPTER EIGHTEEN

IT FELT GOOD. That was the first thing Rosa thought when she woke up. Being home, waking up in her own bed… It felt good. The only thing that was missing was Aaron.

Her second thought was she was going to throw up, followed closely by the fact that she needed to get to the bathroom. She scrambled to it and made it just in time. After a solid fifteen-minute heaving session—her record so far—she brushed her teeth and stumbled into the shower.

The motions of it were so familiar that she had to close her eyes against the tears that burned. Hormones, she told herself. The intense nostalgia—the even more intense regret—were hormones.

It was the only way she could comfort herself. The only way she could lean away from the doubt. She had to believe she'd done the right thing. She *had* to.

She went back to bed after her shower, collapsing there in only her towel. The sun was shining through the glass wall opposite the bed when she clicked to clear the glass, and she almost groaned aloud when its rays hit her body, warming her skin.

She loved the light, the sun in the mornings.

Loved the view of the water rippling out on the dam. She'd missed it. Hadn't realised how much until right that very moment.

Almost as much as you missed the man you shared it with.

A knock on the door interrupted her thoughts.

'Come in,' she called as she sat up. She had no energy for modesty, and was glad when Aaron's face didn't change from its usual unreadable expression when he saw her.

But her heart did soften when she saw that he had a tray with him, and that it held the usual delights for a pregnant woman. Dry toast—butter on the side as an option—and black tea.

'I wasn't sure if you were awake.'

'You didn't hear the retching noises?' she asked wryly, accepting the tray from him.

'No.' He paused. 'Were they bad?'

'No worse, no better.' She took a tentative bite of the toast and, when her stomach didn't recoil after swallowing, took another. 'Though I am beginning to feel like I'm on some cruel reality TV show where this is a delicacy.' She lifted the toast.

'*Torture*—the new show where people who love food are forced to eat only dry toast.'

She smirked, though his words had been said with a straight face. 'Sounds like a winner to me.'

Silence followed her words, and Aaron walked to the window, staring out with his hands in his pockets. He was wearing jeans and a flannel shirt again, and she studied him as she chewed the toast mechanically.

Something about his movements—his posture—worried her. Maybe she shouldn't have mentioned her morning sickness. She knew things like that bothered him.

'I'm sorry. I didn't mean to upset you.'

'You haven't.'

'No?'

He turned. 'Why do you think that you have?'

'Because…' It sounded silly now that she had to say it aloud. She took a breath. 'I know this is difficult for you.'

'What?'

'Seeing me like this.'

'Why?'

'You know why.'

'No, Rosa. I don't think I do.' He walked back to the bed and sat at its edge. 'Tell me.'

She set her unfinished toast aside and took another breath. 'Seeing me sick. It must bother you.'

'It does. But that's because I…care for you,' he finished slowly.

'And because it reminds you of your mother.'

He frowned. 'What?'

'You can't tell me watching me throw up, feeding me this—' she gestured to the toast '—doesn't remind you of how things were when your mother was ill. My mother suffered like that too,' she reminded him softly after a moment. 'I know this is...similar to the reaction to chemo. And that it must be difficult for you.'

Emotion kidnapped his once unreadable expression. It felt like an apt description when Rosa knew he wouldn't have willingly allowed his emotions to show. Nor would he have wanted her to witness it. When he met her gaze, there was a realisation there that stole her breath.

'When you found that lump—when you left— you were thinking about this?'

'I told you that.'

'No, you didn't. Not like this.' He stood. Ran his hand over his head. 'You were worried that if you'd had cancer it would remind me too much of my mother.'

She had to tell him the truth. They were long past the point where she could deny it. She nodded. 'I was protecting you.'

'From myself?'

'From...hurting like you did.' She blinked, surprised at the tears prickling her eyes. 'I saw what your mother's illness did to you. Only realised how bad it was when you started coming out of it. I couldn't do that to you, Aaron. It would have been my fault if I had too, because I chose not to get that test and—'

'And what?' he interrupted. 'If you'd got that test, the result would have changed things?'

'Yes.'

'If it had been negative, maybe. What if it had been positive?'

She had an answer for him. Of course she did. She'd thought all this through. She'd known that not taking that test had been a mistake. Had known it as soon as she'd found that lump.

But when she didn't have the words to offer him, she realised that she'd been fooling herself. That taking that test would have only changed things if, like Aaron had said, the result had been negative. There was no way she'd have been able to stay if it had been positive.

He was right. It wouldn't have changed things.

'I… I need to take a walk,' she said suddenly. 'I need some fresh air.'

He didn't answer immediately, and then he gave her a curt nod. 'I'll come with you.'

'No.'

'Last night you almost fell over in a restaurant. I'm coming with you. Thirty minutes.'

He left before she could respond, and she sucked in air as the door closed behind him. Hoped that somehow the oxygen would make her feel better about what she'd just discovered.

There was no more running from it. She had to face things now. Not only for her own sake, but for the sake of her child. Because she was having a *baby*. And that baby was dependent on *her*.

Her heart stumbled at that, and fear joined tenderness as she finally let herself acknowledge she was going to be a *mother*. She forced herself to breathe, to let air into her body again. And then, when she'd managed that, forced herself to think about her reaction.

This had all started with her own mother. All the things in her life could somehow be traced back to Violet. Rosa's decisions had been dictated by her mother's anxiety, by her illness, and then by her death. She feared making decisions because she could never figure out whether they were right. Because she'd always been torn between what she wanted to do and what she thought she should do. And that was so closely tied to her mother too.

Was it any wonder thinking about becoming a mother herself had caused her to react so strongly?

But when would she stop using that as an excuse? When would she face that *she* made her own decisions now? That *she* lived with the consequences of them?

It didn't matter what her decisions were, she always had to live with the consequences. Good, bad, she had to face them. She was facing them now. The aftermath of leaving her husband. Of conceiving a child with him.

And that last part she couldn't blame on her mother. No, *that* had all been her.

The realisation jolted her. Made her realise the extent of the excuses she'd been making for herself. Her indecisiveness had come from fear—had led to her anxieties—because she hadn't known how to live her life outside of her mother's world.

But, without her realising it, she *had* been living outside of her mother's world. She'd made a life with Aaron outside of it. But she'd left him because she'd blurred the lines between her mother's world and the one she'd created for herself. And it was time that she stopped doing that.

She could no longer use her mother's disease as an excuse not to live her life. She could no longer let it weigh down—or dictate—her decisions. She couldn't let the fear of what had happened to her mother—what might happen to her—turn her into the parent her mother had been.

She took a deep breath as tension tightened in her body. She might know these things now, but living them… That was an entirely different thing.

They were walking in silence.

He wanted to say something to break it, but nothing he thought up seemed good enough. So he waited for her to say something. Waited for her to save him from his thoughts.

They were taunting him. Chiding him. Had kept him awake all night. And now he had the added complication of knowing what she'd meant when she'd said she'd left because of who he was.

It stripped him of every illusion he'd had about himself. And he didn't know how to face it.

'I've missed this,' she said softly, closing her eyes and opening her arms to the sun.

It was so typically Rosa that his heart ached in his chest. Her eyes met his and something jumped in the air between them. And then he looked away, kept his gaze ahead of him, and heard her sigh next to him.

'Don't you get tired of it?'

'What?'

'Thinking so much.'

He almost smiled. 'Always.'

'Then why do you do it?'

'You're saying there's a way *not* to think?'

'Yep.'

'I don't think that's true.'

'Really?' The challenge in her voice made him look over. 'Because I've been known not to think, Aaron. And I have to say I'm pretty good at it.'

Now, he did smile. 'Sure.'

'Remember when I called out that guy who was acting like a complete ass at your end-of-year function?'

'My top paying client,' he offered dryly.

She grimaced. 'Sorry about that. But at least I wasn't thinking.'

'Oh, you were thinking. You just weren't thinking about the consequences.'

There was a beat between them, and he realised that that was exactly what he'd said about his mother. He opened his mouth to take it back, but she was speaking before he could.

'I was thinking that no amount of money should entitle you to treat other people like they're less than you.'

'I think my employees would disagree with you.'

'But *you* didn't,' she challenged. 'You were annoyed at losing him. And yes, I'll give you that. You had the right to be. But you didn't disagree with me. And, if I recall,' she added, 'you replaced him pretty quickly with the guy who helped us get this amazing place.'

She did a twirl with her hands out at her sides. He looked around lazily, enjoying her energy, since it seemed she'd lost some of the fatigue that she'd greeted him with that morning. In fact, he hadn't seen her like this since…since before she'd left.

Neighbours greeted them as they walked, and he nodded while Rosa waved. It was the kind of neighbourhood where people worked from home. Or ran their companies from home, he corrected himself as he took in the borderline mansion properties.

'Hey,' she said suddenly. 'Aren't you supposed to be at work?'

'I pushed my meetings for today.'

'No court?'

'Not today.' He paused. 'The mid-year function is tonight.'

She stilled beside him. 'Are you going?'

'What time is your flight?'

'Seven.'

'It begins at six-thirty.' He considered. 'I probably won't attend then.'

'You're their boss, Aaron. You can't not go.'

'I have more important things to deal with.'

'Like dropping me at the airport?' He nodded. 'No, that isn't as important as this. This…this sets the tone for the rest of the year. And it's been a rough one.' As if he needed a reminder. 'Some might even say it sets *the bar* for your company.' She nudged her shoulder against his.

He chuckled, surprising himself. Though a voice told him he shouldn't be surprised. This was exactly why he'd fallen for Rosa. Because during the worst of times—the most hectic of times— she could make him laugh.

'You have to go,' she insisted softly.

'And who's going to take care of you, Rosa?' he replied.

He'd meant who was going to take her to the airport, but instead the question came out more sombrely than he'd intended. But he realised then that he'd meant the question. And he wanted to know the answer.

Because, since the night before, he'd realised one thing: he was no longer the right person for the job.

CHAPTER NINETEEN

Rosa didn't know how to answer him. Her instinctive response had been that she could take care of herself. But that didn't seem like the best option any more. Not when she wasn't the only one she needed to think about.

Her hand immediately went to her stomach, and she gripped her shirt there. She felt his gaze on her before her eyes caught his, and again something shifted between them. She opened her mouth, but thunder boomed above them and they both looked up.

The sun of that morning was gone and the clouds were now an ominous grey.

'Why does it feel like everywhere we go there's a storm brewing?'

'A metaphor for the way things are between us?'

'Aaron…' She stopped when she saw the smile on his face. Felt her own follow. 'Was that a *joke*?'

'I've been known to make them,' he replied seriously, and her smile grew.

'Really? By who?'

'Everyone.' He looked up when the thunder boomed again, and held out his hand as they turned back. She took it without saying a word. She *de-*

served this, she thought. She deserved this short period that had somehow turned light-hearted. That had somehow turned into a normal day for them.

'Everyone?'

'Everyone. I'll probably get the mid-year award for office jokester tonight.'

She snorted. 'Maybe...*if* everyone who used to work there has been fired and replaced by a bunch of morticians.'

'Are you saying I'm not funny?'

'No. I'm just saying that there are funnier people in the world.' She paused. 'In the country. The city. This conversation.'

She laughed when he sent her a look, and the rest of the walk was in companionable silence. She hadn't expected it, but she was enjoying it.

Though she shouldn't be, she thought. She *had* to speak with him. She had to share what she'd realised earlier that morning. It would entail putting her cards on the table. All of them. Except now, there seemed to be more cards than what she'd started with. Cards she hadn't expected.

Ones that held his laughing face, or the serious expression he'd had when he'd been trying to convince her he was funny. Ones that held that quiet, caring look he'd had when he'd asked her about who would look after her, or the annoyed expression he'd had when she'd said she'd been fine and obviously hadn't been.

Cards that reminded her how in love she still was with her husband.

They arrived at the house just as the sky opened and rain poured down. She settled into the couch as Aaron put on a fire, and felt the tension build as she prepared to be honest with him.

'How are you feeling?' he asked when he sat beside her.

'Okay.'

'Are you sure?'

Something in his voice had her frowning. 'Yeah, why?'

'Because I've been thinking,' he said softly, and her breath caught when she met his gaze. 'And I don't want to think any more.'

In a few quick movements she was on his lap, his mouth on hers.

He shouldn't have done it. And if he had been thinking properly he wouldn't have. But, as he'd told Rosa, he was tired of thinking.

He didn't want to think about how her leaving that evening sat heavily on his chest. Or how he couldn't stop thinking that he needed to convince her to stay. How he couldn't stop wanting to help take care of her, even when he might not be the best person to do so.

He didn't want to think about how close taking care of her and taking responsibility for her were. Or how much that reminded him of his mother.

He didn't want to think about the baby.

He didn't want to think about being a father.

He didn't want to think about *his* father.

He only wanted to kiss her.

And so he had.

She made a soft sound in her throat when their lips met, and it vibrated through him as his mouth moved against hers. As he savoured the taste of her—a fire, a sweetness, a combination of the two that made no sense unless he was kissing her and tasting it for himself.

She shifted so that her legs were on either side of his and tilted her head, both movements allowing their tongues to sweep deeper, allowing their connection to become more passionate.

She kissed without reservation. Without the heaviness that had always weighed each of his actions. The only time he did anything without reservation was when he was with her. When he was kissing her. Because then the only thing that mattered was that he was kissing her.

And that was the only thing he thought about.

About their lips moving in sync, and their tongues taking and giving. About the stirrings in his body, of his heart. Even in this physical act—in the touches, caresses—there was emotion. Memories. Reminders of why he'd fallen for her, and how hard. Reminders of what they'd shared and, now, of what they'd created. Together. Always together.

They were better together.

He fell into the kiss when that made him want to think again, and let his hands roam over the curves of her. He couldn't get enough. Of kneading the fullness beneath her skin. Of the bumps there, the faint feel of her stretch marks beneath his fingers. It had never been enough. It never would be. And so he took, letting his hands speak for him. Letting his touch, his kiss, say what he couldn't.

And when she pulled back, her chest rising and falling quickly, he let his hands linger on her hips, ready to take, to give when she gave the word.

But when her eyes met his he knew that that wouldn't happen. No, the anguish there, the agitation told him so.

'I made a mistake,' she whispered as tears filled her eyes. 'I made a mistake and I don't know how to fix it.'

Let me fix it for you, he thought, but didn't say. Instead, he lifted a hand to her face and let his heart take the lead. For once. 'What mistake?' She shook her head and he took a breath. 'The baby?'

'No.' A tear fell down her cheek and he brushed it away. 'No, not the baby. You.' His throat closed. His breathing stopped. And then she said, 'I shouldn't have left you, Aaron.'

A long time passed as his lungs figured out how to work again.

'How… Why…?'

It was all he could manage.

'I was scared. And I realise that now because

I'm just as terrified. More.' She squeezed her eyes shut and more tears spilled onto her cheeks. 'I left because I thought I was protecting you. But I was just deciding for you.' She wiped her tears away, and his hand fell back down to his lap.

'I have an anxiety problem. Struggling to make decisions—being unable to trust them—is only a part of that. Another is being afraid I'm going to get sick like my mother did. That I'll suffer with being unable to trust my body. That some day it'll betray me anyway.' Her voice had lowered to a whisper again. 'I'm scared, Aaron. I'm scared that this baby will be born into the same kind of world I was born into. That he or she might go through what I went through. That because of me—like me—they'll worry excessively about things they don't have control over too.'

Her eyes lifted to his, the lashes stuck together because of her tears. 'I'm scared that you'll become indifferent to me like my father was to my mother. That this—' she gestured between them '—will never happen again once you realise that the uncertainty, the anxiety—the *sickness*—might not go away. That you'll stop caring.'

She'd barely finished before he pulled her closer, tightening his hold on her. He understood now that leaving him, *protecting* him, had been her way of trying to prevent that he'd stop caring for her.

He hoped that his embrace told her she didn't

have to worry. That he would always care for her. That he'd be there for her whether she was sick or not. And that their kid would be too.

But he knew that this time actions weren't enough. So he loosened his hold and, when she pulled back, took her hands in his.

'You're right. You did make this decision for me and it wasn't the right one.' He paused. 'I know that part of the reason you left was because you thought you were protecting me. But I don't need protection. Not from this.'

'But—'

'Rosa,' he interrupted. 'My mother's sickness hit me so hard because…our relationship was difficult. Finding out she had cancer made me realise she was my only family. So I fought for that.' He took a breath. 'I lost some of myself because of it. I can see that now. But you helped me find that part of myself again. Because of that, I *can* be there for you. Through whatever happens.'

He struggled for his next words, unsure of how to make her see what he saw. 'Everything that happened with your mother was…terrible. But you chose to stay. Even though it was difficult, and you sacrificed a lot because of it,' he said when she opened her mouth to protest. 'Even though now you're still living with the effects of it. You stayed because your mother meant something to you. There's nothing wrong with that.'

She blinked, and another tear made its way down

her cheek. It fell, dropping to his lap before either of them could brush it away.

He wanted to say more. He wanted to tell her that she meant the world to him. That he'd asked her to marry him because she did, and that he'd stand by her side for ever—that he was strong enough to— because that was what he'd vowed to do on their wedding day.

But he couldn't make that promise to her. How could he stand by her side for ever when he knew he wasn't enough for her? When his genes carried things like his mother's flightiness? With his father's disregard for family?

And how the *hell* was he supposed to be a father when the only thing he knew about fathers was that they *weren't* there?

'Aaron?' she asked with a frown. 'What is it?'

The doorbell rang before he could answer.

CHAPTER TWENTY

'YOU HAVEN'T BEEN answering my calls,' Liana said as she brushed past Aaron. She stopped when she saw Rosa on the couch, and then her face split into a smile. 'And if this is the reason, I suppose I'll forgive you.' In three steps she was in front of Rosa, pulling her into a hug. 'It's lovely to see you, darling.'

'Liana,' Rosa said with a smile. Forced, since she was suddenly feeling queasy again, and it was only partly because of her pregnancy. At least she didn't have one of those faces that stayed blotchy for long after crying. 'It's lovely seeing you too. Though I was hoping to see you a month ago. At your birthday party, which turned out to be a ruse.'

Rosa caught Aaron's look of surprise before focusing her attention back on Liana. She had the decency to look guilty.

'It's in the past now, isn't it?'

'Not quite,' she muttered, and then shook her head at Liana's questioning look. 'I wasn't able to give you your gift.'

'Oh, you know that gifts aren't necessary,' Liana said, and then waved a hand. 'Do you have it here?'

'No. I sent it by courier though. It should have been delivered by now.'

'Oh, I haven't been to the house in a while,' Liana replied vaguely, and Rosa wondered whether she should ask. But then, since Liana was there, she figured they'd find out about it soon enough. The expression on Aaron's face told her he figured the same thing.

'How long have you been here, darling?' Liana settled on the couch.

'Just since yesterday.'

Liana frowned. 'But I thought you two…' She trailed off, likely realising that she was opening herself up to another attack by mentioning the island reunion she'd tricked them into. 'Well, then,' she said instead. 'Why haven't you been answering my calls since you got back, Aaron?'

'I was afraid you wanted something,' he replied. 'Since you're here, I suppose I'm right.'

Liana's brows lifted and Rosa felt the surprise echo in her chest. This wasn't the Aaron who dealt with his mother with resignation. Which confirmed her suspicions that something was wrong.

'I didn't realise I was such a burden,' Liana said with a huff. She didn't mean the words, Rosa knew. Liana was more self-aware than she gave herself credit for. She knew her actions burdened Aaron. Though Rosa didn't think she knew how much they hurt him.

'I'm sorry,' Aaron replied curtly. 'You're here for a visit. Do you want me to make some tea? Coffee?'

Liana's expression turned pensive, and Rosa almost smiled at how smoothly Aaron was handling his mother. They all knew now that if Liana said she wasn't there for a visit, she'd expose her lie. So Liana wouldn't come clean, though at some point she'd find a way for Aaron to fix whatever she'd done.

Again, Rosa thought about how blind she'd been to Liana's manipulations. And how much it must have bothered Aaron. How much it must have *hurt* him. But he hadn't shared any of that hurt with her because he'd known how much Liana had meant to her. That was just the kind of man he was.

Rosa would always thank the heavens that Liana had decided Cape Town held the best chances for her recovery. She would always be grateful because it had meant that Liana had been able to make the end of her mother's life better. Liana had done so much for her, for Violet, and Rosa would always love her for it.

But perhaps it was time for her to take her husband's side.

'No, thank you, darling,' Liana said. 'I was just making sure that you were still alive, really. I didn't know what to think after you stopped replying to my messages.'

'I've been busy.'

'Yes. Well.' Liana paused. 'Since you're alive and well, I suppose I can leave. Rosa, it was really lovely to see you. And—' Liana hesitated slightly '—does this mean that I'll be seeing you again in the future?'

'Always,' Rosa answered honestly, and then made a split-second decision. 'Though I was wondering... What are your plans for the rest of the day?' She saw Aaron step forward—to protest, she thought—but ignored him. 'Aaron has a function this evening and I don't have anything to wear. Would you mind taking me to find something appropriate?'

Liana clasped her hands together. '*Of course* I will. I can have Alonso drive us to the boutique immediately. I'll call Kitty. She'll have a couple of dresses waiting when we get there.'

Almost vibrating with glee, Liana took out her phone and went to make her phone calls in the kitchen. When Rosa moved to follow, Aaron caught her arm.

'What are you doing?'

'Being your wife,' she replied simply. 'And doing it the way I should have a long time ago.'

His grip tightened slightly. 'What does that mean?'

'I'm going to accompany you to your function tonight.' It was the easiest explanation.

'What about your flight?'

'I'll change it.'

Or cancel it.

'Rosa,' he breathed, and her name was a warning now.

'Don't worry,' she said, and stood on her toes to give him a kiss. When she pulled back, she saw

Liana watching them with a smug smile. 'Ready?' Rosa asked her mother-in-law, and she nodded. 'See you later,' she told Aaron, and ignored his confusion as she picked up her handbag and followed Liana out of the door.

Rosa had never been a schemer, but when she'd left with his mother that afternoon she'd *definitely* been scheming.

If her answer about why she was doing it was anything to go by, she was scheming for him. And he couldn't figure out what that meant. Or how it made him feel.

All he knew was that her scheming wasn't like his mother's scheming. He trusted that, even if the very fact that she *was* scheming worried him. But Rosa was nothing like his mother. Especially since his mother had never, *ever* done any of her scheming for him.

No, he corrected himself immediately. She had. She was the reason he and Rosa were in this situation in the first place. How had he forgotten that? But then, that made it one scheme for him out of *hundreds* of schemes for other people. So perhaps this one had really only been for Rosa's sake.

He paced the floor, waiting for Rosa to return, and realised why the fact that his mother didn't scheme for him bothered him so much. Because if his mother was going to scheme for him, he wished she'd done so a long time ago.

Like when he'd been younger, and had still cared about growing up in a happy family. When he'd wanted a father, and needed a mother. But none of her schemes had done that. Which told him that she wasn't interested in scheming for him.

Because she'd never wanted him.

Just like his father had never wanted him. And just like he'd thought Rosa had felt when she'd left him.

Now that she was back—now that she'd told him why she'd left—he had to figure out how to get over all the flaws he'd discovered in himself when he'd been trying to figure out why she'd gone.

It left him feeling hopeless. As if he couldn't be a good son, a good husband, a good *father*, no matter how hard he tried.

He choked back the emotion when the door rattled and Rosa walked in. And then a different kind of emotion settled inside him, soothing what had been there before, though he knew it shouldn't.

She wore a royal-blue gown. It had a high neckline adorned with an amazing piece of jewellery, and then creased at one side of her waist before flowing down regally to the floor. The bold necklace was accompanied by matching earrings that he spotted through the spiral of curls around her face.

The colour contrast—the blue of her dress, the bronze of her skin—was striking, and his breath went heavy in his lungs, as if weighed down by her beauty. He'd always been struck by that beauty. It had knocked him down, and then out, and he'd never fully been able to get up again.

It was no different now.

'Are you going to say anything?' she said softly after a moment. Only then did he realise he was gawking at her.

'I...yes. Sorry.' He shook his head. 'You look amazing.'

A small smile played on her lips. 'Thank you.'

'You meant for me to react this way.'

The smile widened. 'Well, I was hoping.' And then faded. 'Just like now I'm hoping that I don't end up being sick in this dress.'

He took a step forward. 'Is there anything I can do?'

'To keep me from throwing up?' She smiled kindly. 'No. But I appreciate the attempt. I'm just going to have to...well, hope.' She paused. 'How are you doing?'

'Fine. Good.' He frowned. 'Why?'

'I haven't seen you all afternoon. Is it a crime to check in?'

'No. But you're checking in for a reason.'

She gave him a look that told him she had no intention of sharing that reason. He bit back a sigh. 'How were things with my mother?'

'Fine. I gave her the opportunity to play fairy godmother with me. Willingly, this time.' She tilted her head. 'Honestly, she loved it. The dress, and then the shoes.' She swept the dress from her leg—nearly stopping his heart as he realised the dress had a slit and he could ogle her leg freely—revealing a shoe that sparkled up at him. She let the dress go. 'Plus, she was thrilled that her plan to get us back together had worked.'

'And you let her believe that.' The dry comment wasn't meant as a question.

'No, actually, I didn't. I told her that she needed to think about her actions. That she wasn't a real fairy, which meant those actions had consequences. And that those consequences affected you.'

He couldn't formulate a reply.

'You're welcome,' she said with a smirk.

'I… I don't know what to say.'

'I just told you you're welcome. You don't have to say anything.'

'Why?' he asked, when his mind still couldn't grasp what was happening.

'Because someone needed to tell her.' She paused. 'I didn't tell my mother that her actions were affecting me. I expected her to know somehow, or I wished… I wished my father would say something. But he didn't, and she didn't, and now—' She broke off on a slow exhale of air. 'I wish I'd said something to her. Maybe our relationship would have changed. Maybe I wouldn't have felt the way that I do now.'

Her eyes had gone distant with the memories, but when she looked at him they cleared. 'So I thought that if I said something to your mother it might make a difference.'

'Did it?'

'She was surprised to hear it.' She bit her lip. The first show of uncertainty. 'She didn't expect anyone to call her out on it.'

'I never did.'

'I know.' She gave him a small sad smile. 'You just did what it took to make it go away. And while I get that—I did it too—it's not going to be as easy to do when the baby gets here. And your mother needs to know that.'

'You told her about the baby?'

'No. I just said that we're working things out, and that that means we have to have boundaries.'

'And she agreed?'

'We'll have to see.' The uncertainty was back. 'Did I...did I overstep?'

'No.' He moved forward and kissed her forehead. 'No, you didn't.' He paused. 'Thank you.'

'You're welcome,' she said again, and rested her head on his chest.

The movement should have comforted him, but instead it sent a ripple through his already unsettled feelings. He wasn't upset by what she'd done, but he also didn't know why she'd done it. Or why it felt as if another weight had been added to what he was already carrying on his shoulders.

CHAPTER TWENTY-ONE

HE WASN'T UPSET with her.

He'd told her he wasn't, and the way he engaged with her seemed to suggest the same. But he'd been distracted on the way to the hotel that was hosting his function. And his usual collected demeanour seemed frazzled.

His colleagues had noticed too. At one point, his partner Frank had spoken about the expansion and Aaron had just looked at him. Had just *stared*. And then he'd asked Frank to repeat the question, and Frank had shot her a look of concern before replying.

Rosa was worried. She was also beginning to think Aaron's strange mood had something to do with her. He'd been that way since they'd kissed that afternoon, and she'd broken down in his lap and spilled her deepest, darkest fears to him. Maybe he regretted what he'd said now.

If he did, would it affect how comforted she'd felt because of what he'd said?

She smiled at one of Aaron's colleagues, accepting their curiosity as a part of the event. She didn't imagine her absence over the past five months had gone unnoticed. And then the previous day she'd shown up at his office and now she was attending the company function.

It was too good to pass up, and so she forgave the people who looked at her as if somehow that would give them the answers they were hoping for.

She focused her attention back on Aaron, but now he was preparing to give his speech for the evening, and he'd gone even quieter. Her chest ached and her stomach rolled, and she pleaded with the new life growing inside her to give her an evening without throwing up. If she did throw up it would no doubt give the people who were looking at her the answers they wanted.

So perhaps they were right to stare at her.

Thankfully, she made it through Aaron's speech. Smart, concise, motivating. He was an excellent boss, she thought, and would make an excellent father.

But was he still interested in being an excellent husband?

The evening moved into a more casual phase after Aaron's speech. The band began to play, the alcohol began to kick in and people were moving to the dance floor. Aaron had been intercepted by one of his employees on his way back to the table, which made it easier for Rosa to excuse herself.

She made her way to the bathroom and then, when she saw the queue to the ladies' room of the venue, pivoted and went to the elevator. She almost pressed for the first floor, but then someone might have the same idea as her, so she pressed for the third floor instead.

It was the top floor of the hotel, and she thanked the heavens when she was able to make it there and locate a bathroom before anyone else saw her. She was also grateful that her baby had allowed her to close the door of the stall before she or he demanded that Rosa be sick.

There was more in her stomach than usual, since she'd felt obliged to eat some of the meal they'd served to avoid suspicion, which made the experience longer and more unpleasant. When she straightened her head started to spin, and she had to spend even more time in the stall to make sure she wouldn't fall over when she exited.

It was all of thirty minutes later by the time she left the bathroom—breath fresh and make-up fixed, thanks to the contents of her bag—and she knew that Aaron would be worried about her. But she still felt a little clammy, and she eyed the door to the balcony before deciding that fresh air might help steady her.

She didn't know what the sound was at first when she got there. Thought it was in her head, the harsh, unsteady breaths. But when her eyes adjusted she saw a shadow in the corner.

She blinked, realised it was a person sitting hunched on the floor, and was about to leave when she realised that that person was her husband.

* * *

He couldn't breathe.

It was the damn tie, and the shirt, and the suit jacket. And though his brain was fuzzy and there were a million thoughts going through his mind—or none—some part of it knew he couldn't throw off all his clothes. So he threw off his jacket, loosened his tie, opened his top button and tried to breathe.

The attempt sounded ragged to his own ears. He was dimly aware of someone else on the balcony and, though he wanted to, he couldn't bring himself to care. If his employees saw him like this it would break something he didn't think could be fixed.

He didn't care.

If Frank saw him it would put their partnership at risk.

He didn't care.

And yet, when he felt the person crouch down in front of him and he lifted his head and looked directly into Rosa's eyes, he found himself caring.

'Rosa,' he rasped. Why did his voice sound so strange?

'It's okay, baby,' she said, settling some of the spinning happening inside him. 'It's okay. You're okay.'

As she wrapped her arms around him he wanted to tell her that it didn't feel as if he was okay. That his head hurt with all the thoughts, and his lungs felt as if they couldn't hold the air he was breathing.

But the thoughts he'd believed so coherent in his mind came out as a garbled mess of air and words. Her hold tightened on him but her voice stayed calm and after some time had passed—he didn't know how long—he looked up at her, and followed her instructions to breathe.

'In,' she told him, 'and out.' She smiled. 'See, you're doing it. Just keep breathing. Inhale on a count to five, exhale on a count to five. You've got this, baby. You can do this. I know you can do this.'

He didn't know how long it took before he believed her. Or how long after he believed her that his breathing actually reflected it. And when he was still—when he felt his mind and body still—she was on her knees and somehow he was cradled in her arms.

'I'm sorry,' he said quietly. She pulled back, her eyes sweeping across his face, and then she shook her head.

'What are you apologising for?'

'That…that you had to see this.' The words were more helpless than he'd intended, and only succeeded in making him feel even more of a fool.

'If by "this" you mean whatever happened out here, don't apologise.' She shifted, and it tugged him out of whatever was going on in his head. The position she was in must have been uncomfortable, and he wasn't sure how long she'd been sitting there like that.

He helped ease her off her knees and then pulled

her forward so that she sat on his lap. She didn't protest, just lifted a hand and swept hair from his forehead.

'You don't have to apologise, Aaron,' she said again, her hand now playing with his hair.

'You shouldn't have—'

'Do you think I wanted you to see me after I threw up yesterday?' She clenched her jaw, and then relaxed it again. After taking a breath, she continued. 'Or have you witness what my anxiety is doing to me? What it *could* do to me?' She lifted her shoulders. 'I've run away—hid—from you before because I didn't want you to see that. But you showed me that was wrong.' She paused, as if she were letting her words sink in. 'Talk to me. Let me in.'

Her words shook him. And again he realised how complicated her decision to leave had been.

But he'd just had a panic attack. The first he'd ever had, and he didn't know where it had come from. He needed time to process that. And what she'd told him. He couldn't find the right words to explain that to her.

'Okay,' she said when the silence stretched. 'Tell me what happened before you came up here.'

'I… I was just talking with Lee about—' He broke off when he realised Rosa would learn nothing about what had caused him to react like that from a discussion he'd had with one of his associates.

Because his panic attack had had nothing to do with what he'd been talking about with Lee. At some point during the conversation his head had started spinning and it had felt as if he couldn't get enough air into his lungs. And his mind…

He'd been thinking about all the promises he'd wanted to make to Rosa, but that he'd never be able to keep.

And about how he couldn't keep lying to her. About how she had the right to know that he wasn't worthy to be her husband. He was barely worthy of being a father to their child.

'Aaron—' her soft voice interrupted his thoughts '—talk to me.'

He looked into her eyes and could only see the things he couldn't give her. 'I can't be there for you, Rosa. Not in the way you need.'

Her heart dipped almost as violently as it had when she'd seen him in that corner. It was still bruised from holding her stoic, strong husband in her arms as he shook, as he struggled for air. It could barely bear the weight of him telling her now he couldn't be there for her.

'I'll get it under control,' she said, her voice just above a whisper. 'No,' she said almost immediately. 'I don't know if I have what my mother had. I don't know if I'm a hypochondriac. Or about the cancer. So I'll get it diagnosed. I'll see a psychologist, and get screened for the breast cancer gene.

I'll keep my anxieties in check. I'm already trying,' she added, desperation fuelling her words. 'I go to the doctor if I feel off, and it almost always *is* something. It isn't in my head.'

The last words were said in a whisper, and her hands reached for his, gripping them tightly. 'I'll fix it, Aaron. Just don't...don't leave me.'

'Rosa,' he said, his voice shaking. But it wasn't from whatever had happened to him. No, it was because of what she'd just told him and she immediately felt guilt crush her.

'I'm sorry. I'm being selfish. I'm being...' The words drifted and she felt tears follow them down her cheeks. 'I'm sorry.'

'I wasn't talking about that,' he replied, and he let go of one of her hands and slid an arm around her waist. 'I should have thought you might think that.' His expression softened. 'That's another part of why you left, isn't it? You thought I'd leave you too. Like your dad did with your mom.'

Not trusting herself to speak, she pursed her lips. Nodded.

'I won't,' he said softly. Firmly. 'Not because of that. Not because of you.' He pressed a kiss to her lips that calmed some of the frantic beating of her heart. 'It's because of me, Rosa. It's always because of me.'

'That's what happened earlier.' Somehow her reaction had made him see the reasons for his own more clearly. 'I was thinking about how I wanted to promise you I'd always be there for you.' He took a breath. Wondered how, over the last month, he'd shared more with her—had delved more into his emotions—than he ever had before.

'Lee's been working on a case where a mother who desperately wants custody of her kids won't get it.' And now that he thought about it—now that his brain was steadier—he realised his discussion with Lee had contributed to his reaction after all. 'She promised them they'd be able to live with her, but her two jobs won't make that possible. She broke down in Lee's office because she'd have to break that promise to them.'

The more he spoke, the clearer it became. 'It's not fair. She works two jobs to make sure that they have everything they want. Except her.' He paused. 'And because of that broken promise they're going to spend their lives not trusting her.'

'Aaron, it's not the same thing—'

'No,' he interrupted. 'That's not what…' He blew out a breath. 'What happened here was partly because of the promise I couldn't make to you, and partly because those kids… They're going to wonder if *they* were the reason that promise was broken. If they did something wrong, or if she really wanted them in the first place.' Emotion, strong and heavy, sat in his chest. 'They're going to be angry with her at first, and then they're going to feel responsible for making sure she believes their existence was worth it.' He looked at her. 'It'll make them take responsibility for things they shouldn't have to. It'll affect their entire lives. And everything that goes wrong from this point in their lives will make them wonder if it was their fault.'

'Like if their wives leave.'

'Yes.'

'Even when it's clear their wives have problems, fears of their own, that contributed to why they left?'

How did she always see what he couldn't say? 'Yes.'

'And at what point do they start believing that there's nothing wrong with them? That their wives love them more than anyone else in the world, and that they would do anything to make them believe that?'

'I'm broken,' Aaron said, and the pain in his chest agreed with him. 'You saw that. You left because of it.'

'But you've shown me that I was wrong, Aaron. The way you've dealt with all this.' She made a vague gesture towards her stomach. 'And with your mom today.' She paused. 'What you said to me this afternoon. You've grown. I just didn't see it.'

'Or you did, and—'

'No, Aaron. I was wrong. Scared.'

'But my mom took so little interest in me, and my dad… He wasn't even there.'

'That's more about them than it is about you,' she

said gently. 'You've learnt that with me this past month.' She squeezed his hand. 'It doesn't mean you're the one who's broken. And if you are… Well, then, all of us are.'

'But your mother and father didn't leave—' He broke off with a shake of his head. 'I'm sorry. I wasn't thinking.'

'No, it's okay.' She leaned back against the railing, making him think about how ridiculous they must look. Her in her beautiful gown, and him in his tux. Broken, shaken, on the floor of a balcony.

'I don't think I ever thought that there might have been something wrong with *me* because my parents…were who they were. Are, I guess, in the case of my dad. Not until I found that lump and freaked out.' She lifted a hand to his face now. 'I understand why you feel this way. And now, with the baby on the way, why it's an issue.'

'Because I'm going to be a terrible father?'

'What? No!' She straightened. 'I meant it made you think of your parents. Of your father. No,' she said again. 'You're going to be a terrific father.'

'I don't know if I can believe that.' He was so tired of saying it, and yet it haunted him so that he couldn't do anything *but* say it.

'Well, I'm telling you.' She paused. 'I know your relationship with your mother is…difficult. And unfair. But she's done a pretty decent job of teaching you how to be responsible.' She wrinkled her nose. 'Silver linings.'

'Yes, I know how to be responsible. I've been responsible my whole life. But look where that got me.' He felt helpless saying it. And, despite what she'd told him, he couldn't believe her. He couldn't believe that he'd be good for them. For her and the baby.

'I'm having a panic attack during a work function, Rosa. I can't face that I'm going to be a father. The responsibility is…easy. I'll look after the child. I'll be there, which is more than what my mom and dad did.' He paused. 'But what is responsibility going to teach this child? That I *have* to love them?'

'Is that how you feel?'

He shrugged. 'I don't know.'

Silence followed his words and, though he knew she would never say it, he sensed that he'd hurt her with his answer. Felt it confirmed when she drew herself up and tried to stand. He helped as much as he could, and was already standing when she turned back to him.

'You have to figure this out, Aaron,' she told him softly, kindly, though he'd hurt her. 'We—me and your baby—don't want to feel like you're just there for us out of some warped sense of responsibility.'

'I wouldn't be.'

'No? There isn't a part of you that feels like the only reason you're open to getting back together again is because I'm pregnant?'

'I… I didn't realise that was on the table.'

She laughed lightly. Mockingly now. 'You didn't

realise that getting back together was an option? Not when I sat on your lap and kissed you back? When I fell apart and told you enough to help you put me back together again?' Any pretence of humour left her face. 'You didn't think me speaking with your mother, me staying here to accompany you tonight, that *any* of that meant I wanted to get back together again?'

'I… I didn't want to hope. After what happened,' he finished lamely.

'After I left.' He nodded, and she sighed. 'Maybe I was stupid for thinking that we'd be able to move past this.' She lifted a hand to her forehead. 'Or maybe we just need to clear it up.' She straightened her shoulders. 'You know why I left. And I know where I went wrong in making that decision.' She paused. 'I'm going to manage my anxiety. Or do my best to try. You said you'd be there for me.' He nodded. 'Did you mean that as the mother of your child, or as your wife?'

He hesitated only briefly. 'Both.'

She gave him a sad smile. 'If this is going to work we have to be honest,' she said, reminding him of his words at the restaurant the night before. But he didn't respond. Couldn't, since he was still trying to figure out what had happened that had got them to this point.

Hope and guilt made a potent shot, he thought, and wondered why he'd downed it.

'Aaron… I want to stay married to you. I love

you—' her eyes went glossy as she said the words '—and I'll always regret how stupid I was to leave you instead of opening up to you. But this whole experience has taught me that there were things that we were going through by ourselves that we shouldn't have gone through alone. That we should have shared.'

She blew out a breath. 'So maybe, in some weird way, this was a good thing.' She went silent, her face pensive, and then she shook her head. 'But we know what we know now. And the actions of the past have brought us here, to make this decision. So, if you want me—' her voice broke and she cleared her throat '—you're going to have to move past what happened and—' she threw up her hands '—and hope again. Because, right now, I'm choosing you again. Not because of the baby. Because of *me*. Because I love you, and I was foolish to believe that I could go through life without you.'

She stepped forward, laid a hand on his cheek. 'But I will, if you can't choose me too. If you don't *want* to be responsible for me and our child. Because that's what it is, isn't it?' She didn't wait for an answer. 'Wanting to be responsible for someone instead of feeling like you *have* to be. Can you say that about us?'

He opened his mouth to agree, to tell her how much he wanted their lives to go back to being how they'd been before. But he knew that he couldn't. Because, as she'd said, they knew what they knew now. And the things he knew about himself worried him more than anything he'd found out about her.

He couldn't be sure that he *wanted* to be responsible for them. Couldn't be sure because he didn't know what *wanting* to be responsible looked like. His entire life had been spent doing things he *had* to do. Except for Rosa. He'd wanted her, but now even that had felt like a compulsion of sorts.

Had he felt obliged to be with her because that had been what their sick mothers had wanted? What her mother had asked of him? Or had it been the attraction, the heat, that had dictated their relationship? Their love?

Her eyes filled again as the silence grew. Her hand dropped and she hung her head. He wanted to comfort her, to draw her in and promise that he'd made a mistake.

He couldn't.

When she looked up at him again her eyes were clear, though there was still that unbearable sadness in them. She lifted up onto her toes, put both hands on his cheeks and kissed him.

It tasted like goodbye, and somehow that taste felt familiar to him. He found himself swept away by it. Felt the emptiness fill him when she pulled away. Felt his hands go to her hips as she lowered to her feet again. As he kissed her forehead.

He didn't know how long they stood like that, but he knew he'd remember for ever what happened next.

'Be happy,' she said hoarsely. 'Find out what that means to you and go for it. I'll be in touch about the baby. We can figure things out once you've had time to…' Her voice faded and it was a few seconds later when she said, 'When you've had time.'

And then she was gone.

CHAPTER TWENTY-TWO

'AND YOU DON'T think it's normal?' The delicate older woman waited patiently for Rosa's reply, and Rosa took a deep breath, preparing herself to answer the question honestly.

She had been the one who'd decided to make good on her promise to get her anxieties under control. She might not have a husband to do it for— she swallowed at the pain that quaked through her body—but she had a child. Or she would have a child. And since her anxiety had spiked since she'd returned to Cape Town the week before, she'd finally decided to go to the psychologist.

'Normal?' Rosa asked. 'The fact that I worry incessantly about what's happening in my body? That I can't trust it?'

'Yes,' Dr Spar replied. 'You don't think, after what your mother went through, it's normal to have your concerns?'

'Well, I suppose that's why I'm here. Because it's normal coming from where I come from.' She bit her lip. 'But the worrying extends to my decisions. And I can't trust them either.'

'Which bothers you?'

'It's affected my life.'

Dr Spar nodded. 'Have you thought about how not trusting yourself might have come from your mother being unable to trust herself?'

'Not quite so specifically. But I know my indecisiveness, or struggling to trust my decisions... I know that's because of my mother.'

'You told me that you didn't want to use your mother as an excuse for your actions any more.'

'That doesn't mean I magically know how to stop doing that.'

'Except being here of your own accord—for your child—means that you have, in some way. Can you see that?'

She lifted a shoulder. 'Maybe.'

'You struggle with it.'

'With seeing that I'm not my mother?' Rosa asked.

'Yes,' Dr Spar replied. 'But also with seeing yourself for who you are.' She paused. 'You're not your mother, Rosa. You can see where your fears and anxieties come from. And you're facing them. Do you think your mother could do that?'

Rosa shook her head silently as she thought it through. The rest of the appointment passed in a blur after that. It had been her second appointment—the first had been spent sharing what Rosa thought she needed help with—but already she knew that it was helping.

She wasn't foolish enough to think she was cured. She was still anxious. Still doubted herself.

And she still couldn't bring herself to be screened for the breast cancer gene, though she was using her pregnancy as an excuse for that. So she made her subsequent appointments and patted her stomach as she walked out of the building.

We're going to get through this, pumpkin, she told her baby silently.

She bit her lip and tried to push past the tears that always seemed to be close by recently. Partly because she'd been worrying about what kind of mother she would be. Worrying that she'd be similar to *her* mother. But having Dr Spar point out how differently she'd reacted to her anxieties compared to her mother had made her feel better.

As she headed home she told herself that it was okay that she didn't want to be like her mother. That she wasn't betraying her mother by wanting that. She'd loved her mother. She wouldn't have put herself through what she had for Violet if she hadn't.

But that didn't negate the difficult experience Rosa had had with Violet. No, that experience and that love could co-exist. And there was nothing wrong with Rosa not wanting her child to live in a world where it did.

It was harder to convince herself that the other part of what had brought her to tears recently was okay. The fact that her child would grow up without his or her parents being together. Especially because Rosa knew how much she'd contributed to that fact.

Her decisions had brought her to this point. Long before she'd found that lump too. And now she knew she'd always fear inheriting her mother's hypochondria. The anxiety, the mistrust of her body, of her decisions, would stay with her.

But she could deal with that. She'd fight for her mental health just as hard as she'd fight for her physical health. Even though that battle would probably extend throughout her life.

She wouldn't let it control her life, her actions. Not any more. She would continue her therapy and learn how to manage it. Learn how to look after herself properly. And see who she really was.

But before she'd got to that point she *had* let it control her life, her actions, her decisions, and she couldn't ignore that she had a part in breaking up her marriage.

She hadn't spoken with Aaron since that night at his work function. She didn't think she was strong enough yet. Not for that. She'd left immediately after that conversation with him. She'd gone back to the house, not particularly caring about what people would say about her departure; she'd packed and had been at the airport an hour later.

The whole thing had cost her a fortune, and there had been no fairy godmother to pick up her tab. But then, her life with Aaron felt like a made-up tale to her now anyway. The clock had struck twelve on her—her carriage had turned back into a pumpkin and she'd turned back into a normal woman with no prince at her side.

'But we don't need a prince, do we, pumpkin?' she murmured softly, laying her hand on her stomach. Ignoring the voice that said, *Liar*.

She *did* need a prince. *Her* prince. But the clock had struck twelve.

She choked back the grief.

It had been two weeks since he'd last seen her. Two weeks without a phone call or message. Of course, he'd gone without either for much longer. But things were different now. Because of the child, he told himself. Because she was pregnant.

Was she okay? Was the baby okay? How was she feeling?

Those questions—and variations of them—had plagued him since she'd left. And he could have got the answers to them with one simple phone call.

That was how he knew he was lying to himself. Things weren't different between them because she was pregnant. At least, not *only* because she was pregnant. They were also different because things had changed between them. Things had become more intense.

He missed her. He missed sharing with her. Regretted how rarely that had happened when they'd been happily married.

Happily.

He didn't think he could use that word any more.

Not knowing what he knew now. Not considering the depths their relationship had sunk to before he'd been stupid enough to let her go.

He took leave from work when he realised his usual strategy of throwing himself into his cases was no longer effective. And if he'd managed to pass off his colleagues' concerns when he'd returned to their function that night two weeks before without Rosa, he wouldn't be able to now. He *never* took leave. And he'd had to convince Frank that he was fine.

But he wasn't.

He spent his days on menial manual tasks. He went to the gym, ran. Fixed things in the house that needed fixing. At some point he found himself at the hardware store purchasing wood, and when he'd got home he'd started building a treehouse. He hadn't given it much thought, had just done it, and he'd been halfway through when he'd realised he was building a treehouse.

Anything to avoid your problems, a voice in his head told him mockingly. But he didn't think he was avoiding his problems. No, he was avoiding his *mistakes*. Because if how miserable he was without Rosa was any indication, he *had* made a mistake. And he didn't know how to fix it.

Which was why he was now at his mother's house.

He had a key, but he didn't want to use it. He'd dodged whatever his mother had wanted because of Rosa the last time, and he hadn't heard from her since. But that didn't mean that he wouldn't. For all he knew, he could be walking into another family staying at his mom's house.

His mind had created such a convincing picture of it that he was mildly surprised when he found his mother alone.

'So, this is the reason for the weather today,' his mother said when she saw him. She stared pointedly out at the rain through the windows before meeting his eyes again. 'You're visiting me.'

'Yes.' He wasn't in the mood for dramatics, though he understood the sentiment. 'I wanted to talk to you.'

'I assumed so, yes. Something to drink?'

When he shook his head she asked for tea from the housekeeper, who'd been hovering in the room since she'd opened the door for Aaron.

When they were alone, Aaron continued, 'What's wrong with me?'

'What?'

'Why didn't my father want me?'

To his mother's credit, she didn't look nearly as surprised as he'd thought she would. Though she did get up and start pacing. When she finally answered him, she had taken her seat again.

'It wasn't you. It was me.' There was pain in her eyes that he had never seen before. 'Your father didn't want *me*.'

'He walked away from his son.'

'Because he didn't want to have a child with me.' She cleared her throat. 'Because he was married.'

'He was...' Aaron couldn't quite process the words, though he'd half repeated them. It took time, during which his mother's tea had been brought and now sat untouched on the table in front of her. 'You slept with a married man?'

'I didn't know he was married when we met.' Liana looked out of the window as she spoke. 'It was a one-time thing too. And when I found out I was pregnant it was hard to find him. The only reason I could was because I had money. Which, thankfully, he didn't know about.'

'He was a one-night stand?' he asked slowly. 'You didn't know him?'

'I was young, Aaron,' she said coolly. 'It was a mistake.'

'You mean *I* was mistake.'

'I've said that in the past, yes.' She looked at him now and her expression softened. 'Though I doubt I meant it. I was just...angry. At myself for making such poor decisions. At you for—' she took a breath '—for reminding me that I should have been responsible.'

'Because I was responsible.'

'Yes.' She brushed a non-existent hair from her face. 'Even though I knew responsibility was your coping mechanism. Responsibility and control.' She smiled sadly. 'Because your mother was irresponsible and out of control.'

'Is that...' He closed his eyes. Opened them. 'Is that why you didn't want to spend time with me when I was younger?'

Her lips pursed. 'I wouldn't have made a good mother. You didn't need me around.'

'I did,' he disagreed softly.

'No, you didn't. Look what's happened to your life since I've been around.'

'It didn't have to be like that. After you got sick—'

'You tried to salvage our relationship,' she interrupted. 'But I saw what that cost you, Aaron.' Her breath shuddered through her lips. 'I said that your father was a one-time mistake, but I've made so many more. I forced you to become someone you shouldn't have had to be. I hurt you beyond measure. I've made you doubt your worth. I'm... I'm sorry.'

He didn't know where her candour was coming from. Didn't know what to do with the emotions it caused inside him. What he *did* know was that his mother's apology meant something to him. That it shifted something inside him.

'You didn't deserve us as parents,' she interrupted his thoughts softly. 'You're a good child. And you have been better to me than I deserved. And your father...' She sighed. 'He's missed out on getting to know you. But that wasn't because of you. That was only because of the circumstances you were born into.'

'Thank you.'

'You don't have to thank me. I should have done this for you a long time ago.'

'Be honest?'

'Yes. And not punished you for my actions. My mistakes.' She leaned forward. '*I* should have been responsible for *you*. Because you were my child, yes, but also because I love you.' She cleared her throat. 'I shouldn't have hurt you the way I have. I should have put you first. I'm sorry.'

'Mom—'

'I knew she'd be good for you,' she interrupted. 'I didn't realise she'd be good for *us*.'

His heart began to sprint. 'Rosa?'

'Of course. She told me all this, you know.' He nodded. 'And she said you'd come here soon. To prepare myself.'

Though his mother's honesty began to make sense now, the reason why surprised him. Again, something shifted inside him. Again, he thought about the mistakes he'd made.

'I see a bit of myself in her.' His eyes lifted and she met his gaze. 'Is that why you're here, and not with her?'

'How—'

'I keep track of my family,' Liana said.

'You knew she was here when you visited me a few weeks ago.'

She nodded. 'I promised Violet that I would look out for Rosa too.'

And yet he was beginning to think that Rosa looked out for them more than they ever had for her.

'She's not like you.'

'No,' Liana agreed. 'She's better. And she's shown you that being spontaneous doesn't have to be a bad thing.' She paused. 'Perhaps she'll help you to let go a little.'

He didn't reply immediately, his mind racing. And finally, when he looked at his mother again, there was a knowing glint in her eyes.

CHAPTER TWENTY-THREE

'WHY DID I decide to live on the top floor of this stupid building?' Rosa wondered out loud, speaking to no one in particular. The elevator of her building had broken. She was almost seven weeks pregnant, and so tired she was barely able to lift a hand to her face, let alone her feet up three floors.

And so she sank down next to the broken elevator, ignoring the looks of the other residents as they easily made the journey up the stairs. She sighed, leaned her head against the wall and closed her eyes.

She was probably going to get mugged. Her handbag was on her lap. The bags from her grocery haul sprawled around her. Toast and tea, ginger biscuits and prenatal vitamins—the extent of what her stomach would hold. And then there were the sample dresses that she'd had to get for her show in two weeks' time.

Why she'd decided to showcase her new line during her first trimester she'd question for ever.

Because you're desperate to prove that you can move forward with your life without your husband by your side?

She groaned, and pleaded with her thoughts to

stop bringing Aaron up. It happened too often for her liking, at the most inopportune times—

'Rosa?'

And now she was hearing his voice. She opened her eyes with a soft curse, and then felt them widen when she saw Aaron right in front of her, crouching down with a concerned look on his face.

'Are you okay?'

She frowned and then reached out, touched his face, to make sure he was really there.

'*Aaron?*'

'Rosa,' he said again, his voice firm. 'Are you okay?'

'If you're really here…' She paused, gave him a moment to confirm it.

There was slight amusement on his face when he nodded.

'Yes, I'm fine.' She straightened now. 'What are you doing here?'

'What are you doing on the floor?' he countered. There was a beat of silence while they both waited for the other to answer, and then she sighed.

'The elevator's broken, and I'm too tired to climb the stairs.'

'That's it?'

'Nauseous, dizzy too. But yes, that's it.'

'So you sat on the floor of an apartment complex?'

She pulled a face. 'I would have moved eventually.' She blew out a breath. 'And yes, I know it's disgusting and I was putting myself in danger, but—'

She broke off when he placed the grocery bags in her one hand, slid her handbag over her shoulder and put the garment bags in her other hand.

'What are you—?'

Again, she broke off. This time, though, it was because he'd scooped her into his arms, holding her as she held the bags easily.

'You're not going to carry me up three floors.' He answered her by turning to the stairwell and doing just that. 'Aaron, you don't have to do this. I'm fine. Just let me down—'

'Are you going to complain the whole way?' he asked, pausing to look down at her. He didn't even sound out of breath, she thought, and cursed him silently for always doing the kind of thing that made her swoon.

'No,' she answered sullenly, and his lips curved. 'It's not funny.'

'No,' he agreed, and kept walking.

Rosa told herself not to get too excited by the fact that he was there. It was probably for the sake of the baby, and she pushed back against the guilt that swelled up inside her. She should have called him, as she'd said she would, and given him an update. But there was no update. She still felt crappy. She still wished that things were different between them.

She couldn't bring herself to call since she didn't

trust what she would say. She'd told him she could live without him that night, but her courage had faltered terribly since she'd left Johannesburg.

Besides, what was wrong with his phone? He could have called her too.

Happy with that, and ready to defend herself if she had to, she barely noticed that they'd reached her floor until he stopped in front of her door and set her down gently.

She stared at him. 'How did you know this was my apartment?'

'My mom.'

Rosa's forehead creased. 'Your mother? How did she… Is that how you knew I was in Cape Town the first time?'

He nodded. 'She always knows where her family is. Her words, not mine,' he said with a shrug when her face twisted into a questioning look.

The day was becoming stranger and, since she didn't want to waste her already limited energy on arguing about something that wasn't worth it, she merely nodded. She handed him the garment bags and reached for the key in her handbag to open the door.

He was still holding the garment bags as he walked in and looked around. She closed the door and tried not to fidget. She lived there, but nothing about the flat was hers. She'd rented it furnished. The quirky colours, odd furniture and weird paintings weren't her choices.

In fact, they'd almost deterred her before she'd remembered the flat had a view of Table Mountain and was located close to the factory that made her designs. She'd realised then that those were her only two priorities.

'Are these for your show?' he asked when she took the bags from him. She didn't bother asking him how he knew.

'Yep.'

'Can I see them?'

'Why would you want to?' she asked tiredly. 'You didn't come all the way here to look at the clothes I designed.'

'No,' he agreed again, and she nearly sighed. Why did he have to be so damn amicable?

'So why did you? Come, I mean.'

'To fight,' he answered slowly.

'What are you fighting for?' she asked after a stunned silence. He'd expected some version of that question, though it was still a punch to the gut.

'You.'

She stared at him. 'There's nothing beyond "you"?'

'I...' He took a deep breath, and then plunged. 'No, there is. I'm sorry, Rosa. For...everything. You shouldn't be here. You should be home. You should be with me.' He gave her a moment to process. 'It's my fault that you're not.'

Her expression remained unreadable. 'How does this change things?'

'I'm here, aren't I?' It came out in a surlier tone than he'd intended. And of course she picked up on it.

'Really? You're annoyed because you're here? Aaron, you've barely said anything beyond *I'm sorry*. And I appreciate your apology, I do, but what am I supposed to do with it? Things haven't changed, which means you're probably here because you think it's what you should do.'

'No,' he said after a moment. 'I'm here because I'm…choosing to be. And because I didn't think about it. I just booked a flight and came here right after I spoke with my mother.'

'You…spoke with your mother?' she asked slowly, before shaking her head. 'No, wait, you *just* booked a flight?'

He clenched his teeth, and then forced himself to relax. 'I was being spontaneous.' He hissed out a breath. 'So yes, I suppose I am annoyed to be here. I'm annoyed that I don't have anything better for you than *I'm sorry*. Because that's what happens when I don't have a plan.'

'But you're here,' she said softly. 'And that means something.'

The emotion in her eyes told him that it did. And suddenly all the uncertainty didn't feel so overwhelming.

'Tell me about the visit to your mother,' she urged softly, when silence took over the room.

'I asked her about… Well, I asked her about my father. And about her.' He cleared his throat. 'About why they didn't want me.'

'And she told you it wasn't you.'

'Yes.' She always knew. 'He was married.'

'Oh, Aaron.' She took a step forward, and then stopped. 'I'm sorry.'

'Don't be,' he said, his heart aching at her hesitation. 'It made me realise that the things I've believed about myself, about my life, weren't entirely correct.'

'And you're okay with that?'

He thought about it. 'No. I don't think I will be for a long time. But I have answers now, and they'll help me figure it out. That's enough for now.' He paused. 'I think that's why you leaving—why all of this—hit me so hard. Because I thought all of it was me. Because I didn't have answers.'

'But you know better now,' she said. 'You have answers.'

'Yes.' He cleared his throat. 'She told me you told her I'd come.'

'A guess,' she said, but angled her face as if she didn't want him to see her expression.

'No, it wasn't a guess.' He walked towards her, stopping only a few metres away. 'You know me. How?'

She laughed hoarsely. 'You're my husband.'

'And you're my wife.' He stepped closer. 'Yet somehow I didn't realise how important that was until you walked away from me. When I saw you again, and I couldn't keep my heart or body from you. And when you told me you were pregnant—'

He sucked in air. Let it out slowly.

'My mother told me she should have been responsible for me because I was her child. But also… because she loved me.' He closed the distance between them now. 'And I love you, Rosa. Being responsible for you and our child… It's because I *want* to be. I'm choosing you.' He lifted his hand, brushed a finger across her lips. 'No matter what happens in my life, Rosa, I always end up choosing you.'

She sucked her lip between her teeth and then blew out a breath. 'You really know how to sweep a woman off her feet, don't you?'

His lips curved. 'I'm only interested in sweeping one woman off her feet.' His hand dropped to her waist. 'You have questions.'

'So many,' she said on a little outburst of air. 'But I also have to tell you… I've been seeing someone about my anxiety.'

'Has it been helping?' he asked carefully.

'Yes. But it's not just going to go away.'

'I know.' He took her hand. Squeezed. And let go.

'And I haven't done the test yet.'

'The screening?' She nodded. 'Can you do it while you're pregnant?'

'I... I haven't seen a doctor about it, so I don't know for sure. But I wanted you to know, so that—'

'I can be there for you if and when you choose to go?'

Her mouth opened, and then she swallowed. 'I'm going to do it.'

'Okay.'

'So there's no *if*.'

'Okay.'

Her brow furrowed. 'You're really okay with all this?'

'They're your decisions, Rosa. I'll support you, no matter what you decide. And we'll deal with the consequences of whichever decision you make.'

Her eyes filled. 'Thank you.' Seconds later, she said, 'You mean it, don't you?'

'Yes.'

'You're choosing it. You're choosing me.'

'Rosa, I had a heart-to-heart with my mother about my father, and her actions in the past.' He stroked her hair. 'And then I flew here on the spur of the moment with only my mother's word that you'd be here. I have no clothes, no toiletries, no place to stay. I only have you.'

'But—'

'I don't want to waste my life like my parents did,' he interrupted. 'Their choices—the fact that I'm here—were a series of mistakes. And yes, we've made mistakes too. But *we* were never a mistake.'

His hands moved to her waist again, and tightened there. 'And, if you'll have me, I'll believe that nothing that's brought us here has been a mistake either.'

Now he placed a hand on her abdomen and felt his entire body warm when she covered his hand with both of hers.

'I still love you, Rosa,' he said again, quietly. 'I've never stopped—'

He was silenced by her lips on his. It was a long, sweet kiss, free from the anguish that had plagued them for longer than either of them knew. Only when the doorbell rang did they come up for air.

'I'm not expecting anyone,' Rosa said breathlessly as she moved to open the door. He caught her waist.

'I am.'

'What? Who?'

'I...ordered some camellias.' He swallowed. 'I remember you said you liked them. I know they're not your favourite, but they're sometimes called the rose of winter.' He waited nervously but she didn't say anything. 'If we have a daughter,' he added quickly, 'the name would be perfect to fit into your family's tradition. Because yours is Rosa, and she was conceived in—'

Again, she silenced him with a kiss. Tears glistened on her face when she drew back. 'I... I can't tell you how much that…' She stopped, offering him a watery smile. 'Thank you.' She laid her head on his chest. 'I love you, Aaron.' She paused. 'We're going to figure it all out, aren't we?'

He kissed the top of her head. 'Together.'

She looked up at him and smiled. 'Together.'

* * * * *

If you enjoyed this story,
check out these other great reads
from Therese Beharrie

Tempted by the Billionaire Next Door
Falling for His Convenient Queen
United by Their Royal Baby
The Millionaire's Redemption

All available now!

COMING NEXT MONTH FROM

♦ HARLEQUIN™

Romance

Available September 4, 2018

#4631 ENGLISH LORD ON HER DOORSTEP
by Marion Lennox

Stranded with handsome stranger Bryn Morgan during a storm,
Charlie can't help seeking one night of comfort in his reassuring arms...
The two forge a seemingly unbreakable bond—until morning brings the
revelation that Bryn is in fact Lord Carlisle!

#4632 THE MILLION POUND MARRIAGE DEAL
by Michelle Douglas

Billionaire playboy Will Trent-Paterson has just one year to get married.
And his old friend Sophie Mitchell has the perfect temporary solution:
she'll marry him—for one million pounds! Only, Will soon realizes walking
away from captivating Sophie isn't going to be easy...

#4633 CONVENIENTLY WED TO THE PRINCE
by Nina Milne

When Prince Stefan learns he might inherit land in his estranged
principality, he discovers beguiling Holly Romano is also named in the
will—and the land goes to whomever marries first... So they join forces
and conveniently marry *each other*!

#4634 THE ITALIAN'S RUNAWAY PRINCESS
by Andrea Bolter

With her arranged royal wedding only weeks
away, Princess Luciana flees to Florence for a
glimpse of life outside the palace walls...only to
be rescued by guarded billionaire Gio Grassi!
Could this chance encounter change the
course of their lives—forever?

YOU CAN FIND MORE INFORMATION
ON UPCOMING HARLEQUIN® TITLES,
FREE EXCERPTS AND MORE AT
WWW.HARLEQUIN.COM.

HRLPCNM0818

Get 4 FREE REWARDS!

We'll send you 2 FREE Books plus 2 FREE Mystery Gifts.

FREE
Value Over
$20

Both the **Romance** and **Suspense** collections feature compelling novels written by many of today's best-selling authors.

YES! Please send me 2 FREE novels from the Essential Romance or Essential Suspense Collection and my 2 FREE gifts (gifts are worth about $10 retail). After receiving them, if I don't wish to receive any more books, I can return the shipping statement marked "cancel." If I don't cancel, I will receive 4 brand-new novels every month and be billed just $6.74 each in the U.S. or $7.24 each in Canada. That's a savings of at least 16% off the cover price. It's quite a bargain! Shipping and handling is just 50¢ per book in the U.S. and 75¢ per book in Canada*. I understand that accepting the 2 free books and gifts places me under no obligation to buy anything. I can always return a shipment and cancel at any time. The free books and gifts are mine to keep no matter what I decide.

Choose one: ☐ **Essential Romance**   ☐ **Essential Suspense**
                         (194/394 MDN GMY7)   (191/391 MDN GMY7)

Name (please print)

Address   Apt. #

City   State/Province   Zip/Postal Code

Mail to the **Reader Service:**
IN U.S.A.: P.O. Box 1341, Buffalo, NY 14240-8531
IN CANADA: P.O. Box 603, Fort Erie, Ontario L2A 5X3

Want to try two free books from another series? Call 1-800-873-8635 or visit www.ReaderService.com.

*Terms and prices subject to change without notice. Prices do not include applicable taxes. Sales tax applicable in NY. Canadian residents will be charged applicable taxes. Offer not valid in Quebec. This offer is limited to one order per household. Books received may not be as shown. Not valid for current subscribers to the Essential Romance or Essential Suspense Collection. All orders subject to approval. Credit or debit balances in a customer's account(s) may be offset by any other outstanding balance owed by or to the customer. Please allow 4 to 6 weeks for delivery. Offer available while quantities last.

Your Privacy—The Reader Service is committed to protecting your privacy. Our Privacy Policy is available online at www.ReaderService.com or upon request from the Reader Service. We make a portion of our mailing list available to reputable third parties that offer products we believe may interest you. If you prefer that we not exchange your name with third parties, or if you wish to clarify or modify your communication preferences, please visit us at www.ReaderService.com/consumerschoice or write to us at Reader Service Preference Service, P.O. Box 9062, Buffalo, NY 14240-9062. Include your complete name and address.

STRS18